THE BILLIONAIRE'S SECRET CHRISTMAS HIDEAWAY

A SECRET BILLIONAIRE ROMANCE

KIMBERLEY MONTPETIT

KIMBERLEY MONTPETIT

The Secret Christmas Hideaway

THE BILLIONAIRE'S CHRISTMAS HIDEAWAY: A SECRET
BILLIONAIRE ROMANCE

Spellbound Books

Published in the United States of America

Copyright © 2022 by Kimberley Montpetit

All rights reserved.

No part of this book may be reproduced in any form or by any
electronic or mechanical means, including information storage and
retrieval systems, without written permission from the author,
except for the use of brief quotations in a book review.

Fall in love all over again in a small town at Christmas!

CHAPTER 1

The phone was ringing off the hook despite Revé Chatham's two quite capable secretaries in the well-appointed outer office. But these days, nearly every call was one that Revé had to field with questions only she could answer.

Chatham Pharmaceutical had just released a new cancer-busting drug and if it wasn't the hospital administrators, oncologists, or nurses calling for details about availability or administering the long-awaited medicine, it was patients or their relatives from clinics around the world. Revé even had three translators working the phones.

"Perhaps two weeks before Christmas wasn't the right time to launch the new drug," she muttered to herself, typing her thoughts, ideas, and information on multiple notepads on the computer screen as fast as she could.

Her desk was also a mess of scribble, and a headache was coming on strong. It was after six already, and she was starving. Had she even had lunch?

A fresh call came in, and Revé flipped through her calendar to glance at a few upcoming meetings. It was too bad her father, Milton Chatham, was up north in San Francisco right now at a meeting with the heads of their manufacturing plants reworking production schedules, especially with so many employees on vacation during the upcoming week of Christmas.

December was normally a slow time of year—which is why her father had initially decided to launch the new drug after receiving approval through the FDA at last—after more than a decade of testing. Oncologists had been waiting for this new drug for a long time.

Because Revé had a nursing degree along with her MBA, her father had put her team in charge of taking calls from doctor's offices, including conference calls with clinics around the country.

Thank goodness, she had two medical doctors with chemistry degrees on her staff to field the more technical inquiries, including their role in functioning as the liaison between the three Chatham laboratories.

The new drug was an exciting advancement in blocking cell receptors that liked to "hide" the cancer in someone's body. Being able to detect the growing cells or predicting where they were meant having the ability to destroy them permanently and the hope that a patient would then go into full remission that could last for years, or a lifetime.

The response had been astounding, and was incredibly gratifying as well.

Revé's head of staff, Alexa Wilson, poked her head in the door, raising her eyebrows in case Revé was on a conference call.

"Just finished the last call of the day," Revé said with a wave of her hand. She leaned back in her chair and punched off the phone. "Must be Friday, the calls and meetings have been non-stop. Can we go home yet?"

"Afraid not, Ms. Chatham. Your father called while you were on the line and said that he's got a meeting set up for you with Dalton Bennett, the director of Presbyterian Hospital across town—including his staff."

"But my father usually does those," Revé said, puzzled. "Why didn't he schedule it for next week when he returns?"

"Because Mr. Bennett insisted it had to be tonight. They have someone in town from Chicago that leaves tomorrow and want a personal meeting before signing the contract with us. A *huge* shipment is on the docket, and we may need to reallocate a special shipment just for them. So, you need to wow them. Your father's words, not mine," Alexa added with a smile.

"But I'd planned to go Christmas shopping," Revé

muttered. "And you know I'm supposed to leave for India with my mother and brother's family in two days. Tonight is also my special Christmas date with Warren, and I need to pick up his gift at the tailor before they close."

"I'll grab it up for you while you meet with Dalton Bennett—and I'll even place a giant red bow on the new leather jacket, too."

"I can't ask you to do that," Revé said with a wan smile, rubbing her tired eyes. "You're always doing nice things for me."

Alexa gave a little laugh. "Hey, I only have cats at home, they can wait an extra hour for their tuna. Seriously, I don't mind, and you look beat."

"That bad, huh? Gee, thanks."

"Nothing that a full eight hours of sleep won't cure. You're always gorgeous, even when you're exhausted."

"You're too sweet, Alexa, what would I do without you? But I'm starving now. . . can I sneak in some Chinese take-out?"

Alexa shook her head. "No can do. You need to leave in about thirty minutes."

Revé's fingers hovered over her computer keyboard. "Why on a Friday night? Don't doctors have families, too?"

Alexa shrugged. "Hospital board presidents are a different breed, despite being doctors themselves. Director Bennett wanted to meet with a Chatham executive personally about ordering larger than normal quantities for their new cancer center that just opened. They're raring to go on several new patients with their team of oncologists."

Revé flipped through her calendar, a knot of panic rising in her throat. "What day *is* it?"

"Friday, the fourteenth."

"It's been such a frantic week I'm still looking at Thursday's schedule, what an idiot I am!"

"Do I need to turn your calendar every day now, Miss Chatham?" Alexa teased.

"That's probably not a bad idea—at least until we get through the holidays," Revé said drily. "I swear I'm losing my mind."

"Don't forget that you're leaving all this insanity behind on Tuesday when you fly to India. All problems, emergencies and questions will be routed through to the board members and our doctors on call until after the New Year."

When the mention of India came up—the birthplace of her mother—Revé's gut tightened. She'd always looked forward to their annual trip as a family, but this year a reluctance had settled on her. Maybe it really was just fatigue. The plane ride alone was enough to over-dose on sedatives.

Shaking her head, Revé finally jumped to her feet. She only had twenty minutes to get there. "Are you sure I can't put this off until later?" she asked.

Alexa shook her head. "Not a chance. Now go change into a nice dress and freshen your lipstick. Doctor Bennett made reservations at The Markus."

Revé gave a quick laugh. "And I'm supposed to be impressing *them*? Wow, I think they're trying to impress us. Do I have enough calories left today that I can order the filet mignon?"

"Absolutely. And add their to-die-for shrimp scampi. I don't think you've eaten all day, except for those Doritos and Fiesta Green Chile dip your friend, Carmen, from New Mexico sent you."

"That dip *is* divine, isn't it? I couldn't stop eating it until my mouth was burning with ecstasy."

"I've heard green chile has addictive qualities—that's why you can't just eat one."

"Seriously? Huh. Okay," Revé said, rushing around her office. "Where'd I put my dress and heels?"

"Right here." Alexa held up the hanger with her black dress in one hand and the straps of her dress shoes in the other.

"You are a lifesaver!" Revé gushed.

"I'm going to officially change my middle name to 'lifesaver,'" Alexa joked, opening the door to the private restroom in Revé's inner sanctum.

Revé knew she was spoiled. Her father, Milton Chatham, had remodeled the offices the previous year and it was so charming.

Revé hadn't grown up with her family's current

wealth, but the last ten years since she'd finished grad school her parent's pharmaceutical company had exploded with success and new research, so she and her older brother now had stuffed 401K's and bank accounts.

Being a wealthy millionaire—or *billionaire*—was still a little strange. It made her self-conscious, but her parents were such genuine people who gave so much to various charities that it kept them all grounded, for which Revé was grateful. The wealth of her family was a little embarrassing, and she tried not to think about it.

Her mother's family in India were neither poor nor well-off, but the aunties and uncles and cousins were grateful for college funds provided by their Uncle Milton and Aunt Anya, and her grandmother was in love with her new kitchen appliances.

"You look gorgeous, Revé," Alexa gushed when she re-entered the office.

Bending down, she slipped into her heels and twirled. "Nothing untoward showing? No slips or cellulose?" Revé asked with a quirk of her eyebrows.

"You look perfect, as always. The only question is whether the doctors and hospital administrators you're meeting are old dudes or handsome young guys that will sweep you off your feet."

"Unfortunately, I have already been swept off my feet —by Warren Dailey." Revé said gaily, bubbles of anticipation rising in her stomach. "I think Warren may propose sometime over the holidays! I caught him hinting at a surprise for me over the phone one day to his best friend, Paul."

"I knew it, I knew it," Alexa said, giving her hand a quick squeeze. "It's so exciting and romantic—an engagement at Christmas! Making out under the mistletoe!"

Revé laughed, searching for her handbag to head out the door.

"Right here," Alexa said, dangling the purse from her fingertips.

"Don't know what I'd do without you," Revé told her, rolling her eyes at herself. "I'm not usually this distracted."

"Your mind is elsewhere—on a certain man who may be picking up a diamond ring at this very moment and getting it gift-wrapped to put under the Christmas tree."

"Oh, you," Revé said, shaking her head. "You're too much. Now stop, the entire idea might all be in my head and merely a daydream."

"I have a taxi waiting for you downstairs."

"I can't leave my car in the parking garage. How will I get back to work in the morning?"

"First off, tomorrow is Saturday, and if you show up to work, I'll strangle you. Second, I'll get Brad to help me drop your beloved Maserati at your house. You don't want to be fighting for a parking space so close to Christmas or distracted by bad traffic. Go—be calm—

dazzle the hospital president with what Chatham Pharmaceuticals can do for them."

Revé gave Alexa a brief hug and finally took the elevator down to the lobby. As promised, there was the yellow taxicab waiting for her.

She slid into the vehicle, and the driver said, "The Markus, ma'am?"

"That's right," she replied, "Thank you."

It was strange to be called "ma'am," but she was well over thirty now and the fact seemed to act like a beacon to all strangers that she was no longer a "young thing."

Was that why she'd been feeling a bit out of sorts—while hiding her trepidation from Alexa and her parents who were already packed to go to India. Revé hadn't even begun to pack, and she refused to let Alexa do that for her, too. She didn't want to be like a spoiled heiress.

But Revé longed for something different. She was tired of L.A. Why couldn't she have a white Christmas for once, not hot and muggy India, even though she adored her grandmother's holiday cooking—the Allahabadi cake and melt-in-your-mouth tandoori chicken.

Despite enjoying her huge extended family, she'd gone to India only six months ago for a cousin's wedding.

Maybe it was leaving Warren for two weeks, especially if she was wearing his ring on her finger. Maybe, maybe, maybe—she didn't know!

Getting the folder out of her briefcase, Revé frantically glanced at her notes for the dinner meeting, including the answers to potential questions. She wished her father was going to be in attendance. He was so good at these things, smooth and unflustered.

Revé took a deep breath when the taxi pulled up in the circular drive of the restaurant in downtown Los Angeles.

Christmas lights were strung along the perimeter of the restaurant, holiday shoppers streaming across the sidewalks. Only ten shopping days left!

Two weeks was a long time to be gone from Warren—and that, she had to admit—was the entire reason for her unsettled emotions. And fear.

Over the last ten years of her life, she had almost married two other men and both relationships ended badly, her heart broken into pieces. Betrayal by her college love, Gary, and then total indifference when Martin deserted her a month before the wedding.

That was an expensive break-up—and embarrassing when her family had to get on the phone and call everyone who had received the announcement to tell them the wedding was off. Returning the gorgeous satin dress she'd special-ordered, the glittering diamond ring, cancel the catering, the Hotel Monaco for the reception —all of it was soul-ripping.

Thankfully, her old friend Carmen jumped in to rescue her and took over the long list of cancelations, sparing Revé from the embarrassment.

There were days Revé was sure she was cursed when it came to her romance life.

Revé tut-tutted to herself, recognizing her mother's funny habit. How ridiculous she was being! Paranoid! Nothing was going to happen to safe, perfect Warren. *He* was The One. They'd have a beautiful summer wedding on a sunny day next June.

Sliding out of the taxi, she handed over three twenties, wished the driver a Merry Christmas, and hit the sidewalk with her high heels, gripping her briefcase firmly in one hand.

"Right now, focus on the dinner and your clients," she told herself sternly.

When Warren had texted to arrange a meet-up for drinks after her business dinner meeting, her stomach had jumped with anticipation. Perhaps *tonight* was *the night* after all. Was a proposal finally going to happen?

Revé glanced down at her left hand, picturing a diamond ring sparkling on her finger in a few hours. When the doorman opened the double glass doors to The Markus, a secret smile played on her lips.

CHAPTER 2

"How was your dinner?' Mr. Bennett, the president of Presbyterian Hospital, asked as he ordered a plate of various bite-sized desserts for the table.

His assistant, Madison Sampino, a mild-mannered woman who had been taking notes all evening in between bites of her salad or baked chicken, took a sip of her wine and finally sat back.

Inwardly, Revé grinned, as if Ms. Sampino was finally off the clock and could relax. "The filet mignon and shrimp scampi were perfect, as usual, although I haven't been here in at least a year."

"You need to come more often, Miss Chatham," Madison told her. "The menu is so large, it would take months to try all their entrees."

"Very true," Revé agreed with a small laugh. "I'll

encourage my father to bring our entire office here for a Christmas dinner next week before we leave for New Delhi."

"Yes, please," Mr. Hale, the hospital supervisor over its Cancer Center said, nodding at the waiter to refill everyone's water and wine glasses from a fresh bottle.

The ice in the water decanter clinked together, and soft instrumental Christmas music made a lovely background to the restaurant which was decorated in sparkly red and white pine trees and wreaths.

Revé's smile suddenly froze on her lips when, out of the corner of her eyes, she saw her boyfriend Warren being seated by the maître'd at a table across the dimly lit room. A stunning blonde woman was with him, coyly turning her head to look up at him.

Revé set down her water glass with trembling fingers, choking as she tried to swallow.

"Is everything all right?" Ms. Sampino asked, a look of concern on her face.

"Fine, I'm perfectly fine," Revé stuttered, waving a hand in the air. "Just swallowed wrong." She gulped and pressed her linen napkin to her lips, staring daggers at Warren and the woman he was with. *Who was she? What was he doing?*

Her heart pounded so ridiculously hard, she feared the entire table would hear it above the Christmas music.

Furtively, she propped her cell phone against her

water glass on the table as though looking into a mirror to touch up her lipstick—while pressing the button on the camera's video with shaking fingers, at the exact same moment that Warren placed a hand over the woman's arm in an intimate gesture.

The sight of the man she loved with another woman in an intimate seating arrangement sent her blood pressure rising. Her face turned hot, but her own dinner companions were watching her.

She took a breath, trying not to panic. "Mr. Bennett, Mr. Hale, do you have any other questions I can answer?"

Inside, her mind was whirring with her own questions. Perhaps the woman was Warren's sister, Emily, who was expected in town from Florida for the holidays. She'd caught an earlier flight or something.

Except Revé knew in her heart that this woman in her clinging red dress with blonde tresses flowing down her back in big, bouncy waves, wasn't Warren's *sister*.

They leaned close, whispering, giggling, attempting to look at their menus while continually being distracted by each other.

The woman scooted her chair closer to Warren's, linking her fingers through his and whispering something into his ear. Warren blushed, gazing into her eyes and kissing the back of her hand while Revé gritted her teeth, frozen in place like she'd turned to ice.

It was clear her boyfriend was not on a business

dinner. All the sounds in the restaurant seemed to stop, and there was a loud rushing sound in her ears as if she'd gone deaf.

Warren had never brought her to The Markus so he probably never expected Revé to be across the room. He appeared perfectly at ease, not guiltily glancing about to make sure he didn't know anyone there.

Discreetly, she kept the video recording going but it was maddening to keep it aimed in the right direction while she tried to chat with her dinner companions when the dessert tray arrived.

Bite-sized cheesecakes, miniature chocolate lava cakes, and baklava lay arrayed in crinkled green paper cups, but Revé couldn't seem to focus. Her eyes glazed while the rest of the table made noises of delight at the exquisite delicacies.

Revé mindlessly nodded like a robot while the rest of her group chatted about family holiday traditions and vacation plans now that their business had concluded. It was all she could do to sit still and not run screaming from the room. Instead, her eyes were glued to the scene taking place across the room at her boyfriend's table.

Warren slipped a hand into his pocket and pulled out a small white jewelry box. When he popped it open, a dazzling diamond ring sparkled under the restaurant lamps. The woman put a hand to her ample chest with its plunging neckline in a surprised gesture.

Warren was proposing to her! Revé thought she would be sick.

Warren took the ring out of the box and slipped it onto the blonde woman's finger, leaning in close as if nibbling on her ear.

The woman's sultry laugh wafted through the dining room while she admired the diamond ring on perfectly manicured fingers.

Wearing the diamond engagement ring and clutching it to her breast, she scrambled to her feet and came around to his side of the table, bending Warren's head back to place her mouth on his in a long and sensuous kiss.

Fighting to keep the tears from spilling, Revé thought she might throw up.

The woman continued to wear the ring while their salads arrived. Most likely she would wear it until Warren left to meet Revé for drinks to break up with her.

Revé pushed her plate away, gulped at her water and slipped her cell phone back into her evening purse.

"Are you feeling all right, Ms. Chatham?" Mr. Hale asked. "You look a little pale."

"Probably these dusky lights," Madison said, giving Revé a small smile.

Revé mumbled something in agreement, forcing herself to act normal despite the fresh headache. "A little tired," she admitted. "It's been a wild month with the new drug going out across the world—and I still need to pack to leave on Tuesday for India." She added a little laugh to lighten the mood.

"Ooh, India, I've always wanted to travel there," Madison said.

"It's just home to me—in many ways. I've been going every year to see my mother's family since I was born."

"I can imagine it will be a splendid holiday for you all," Mr. Bennett said. "Chatham Pharmaceuticals has done well. Our doctors and hospital administrators are so pleased to finally have the FDA approval and we're looking forward to some wonderful results for our patients."

"The decade of testing attests to that," Revé replied, forcing the words to come out naturally and with confidence. "It has been one of our most rewarding research projects."

"Well," Madison said, pushing away from the table. "I know it's only nine-thirty here in California, but I'm going to call it a night. I'm jet lagged out here on the west coast, it's almost midnight for me."

Gratefully, Revé rose too, snatching at the opportunity to leave, too. Her eyes kept darting over to Warren and the blonde hussy. *She* was the one that was supposed to be meeting him in less than an hour. All day Revé had been hoping that she'd be getting a ring tonight. A string of curse words ran through her mind.

"I'm going to visit the ladies room," she said vaguely.

"May I call a cab for you, Revé?" Mr. Hale asked, his fatherly white hair and gentle voice comforting.

"Thank you, but I'll be fine. I may call my brother, we have, um, family trip details to work out."

Mr. Bennett reached out to shake Revé's hand. "Thank you for everything and for taking the time to meet with us before the holidays. We can move into the New Year on the ground and running."

"Our pleasure," Revé assured him, clutching her briefcase, a fresh file of paperwork and physician names on a list he'd given her. "I'm just sorry my father is in San Francisco right now."

"We'll be in touch, have a safe and wonderful holiday," Mr. Bennett added.

Revé gave a little wave as she moved quickly to the rear hallway and the ladies room. Leaning back against the wall, she took deep, shaky breaths, making sure the camera on her phone had turned off.

Placing cold hands against her hot face, sobs rose in her chest, but she had to get herself in control. She couldn't run crying from The Markus.

At the same time, hot fury clawed up her throat. How dare Warren propose to that woman before he'd officially broken things off with her! The nerve! The gall!

It was worse. Warren had been carrying on with both of them at the same time.

If they had been married, Revé would have marched

herself straight off to a family attorney and sued him for everything he owned.

Instead, she smoothed her black dress and marched back into the main room of the restaurant. The city lights of Los Angeles sparkled through the plate glass windows, but she kept her eyes riveted to Warren Dailey, traitor and cheater—for he apparently had been cheating on her for a very long time.

At least all the other loser men in her life had broken up with her before they ran off with someone else. Not Warren—the one man she had trusted for the first time in so long!

Striding closer to Warren's table and the woman with her perfect blond curls and bursting bosom, Revé's face was so determined that other diners glanced up as she passed, curiosity in their faces.

When she got within five feet of Warren, he suddenly jerked his head up and saw her. The color drained from his face. Half-rising to his feet, he spluttered, "Revé—it's —what are you doing here?"

"Isn't that the question *you* should be answering, you jerk?" Without another word, Revé lifted his glass-cut pitcher of ice water and dumped it over his head.

He gasped at the shock of the water, and Revé saw with satisfaction that it would probably ruin his suit— and her further achievement was when the water splashed against the woman's fancy evening dress, too.

Gasping with indignation, her face turned bright red.

"Are you some crazy woman?" she snarled. "Warren, you should sue this insane person—how dare you?"

"How dare me?" Revé said, watching dribbles of water run from her hair, flattening it from its perfect coif and hairspray. "Ask Warren, your lover-boy. He's got all the details. You'd just better hope your diamond is real."

"You insulting, impudent witch."

Her face burning, Revé held back the urge to whack the woman across the head with her briefcase.

The rest of the restaurant patrons were now fully staring at them, and the volume of murmurs and chatter rose in the dining room.

The maître'd hurried over, worry creasing his face as he snapped his fingers at two of the waiters to retrieve towels.

"Revé," Warren said, his voice hard and cold. "I could sue you for damages. You have no idea what's going on here. Don't jump to conclusions."

"Go right ahead and try suing me, Warren," she answered just as hard and cold. "I recorded it all right here on my camera so don't try to threaten me. If you do, I'll make your life miserable and your fake blonde fiancé run far, far away."

Warren's face fell as he realized that Revé was right.

Spinning on her heels, Revé headed for the restaurant's exit. She'd been humiliated by Gary and Martin before, but for the first time she'd done something to fight back, and it felt good, really good.

When she glanced up, she spotted Madison Sampino standing at the far end of the marbled foyer of The Markus. The woman gazed at Revé with a look of astonished wonder and admiration.

Revé's face heated. Oh, what had she done! Her father would be furious that she had acted so childishly and irresponsible in front of their hospital customers.

The rest of the patrons waiting in line to be seated were a blur as she headed blindly for the door.

Ms. Sampino was suddenly at her side. "Brava, young woman," she whispered with a light touch on Revé's shoulder. "I saw the entire thing. I could tell you were recording something with your phone, and it soon became apparent who you were glaring at."

Revé bit at her lips. "Oh, dear, was it that obvious?"

The woman shook her head conspiratorially. "Only to another woman. Now go home and forget that louse. He's not worth it."

CHAPTER 3

Her triumph lasted until Revé arrived back at her apartment in a drizzling rain. The realization of what she had done came over her like a punch in the stomach. *She'd thrown a pitcher of water at Warren in the middle of The Markus, one of the most elite restaurants in Beverly Hills.*

Even though she had ignored the shocked patrons— she'd never be able to show her face there again.

The rest of it was a blur. Had Mr. Bennett and Mr. Hale still been standing there? Had their two major clients seen the entire scene like Madison Sampino had?

Revé's face burned. "What have I done?" she moaned, burying her face into her pillow.

But that's wasn't the worst of it. Warren, her boyfriend of the past two years, who she had been persuaded was about to propose, had cheated and betrayed her in the worst possible way.

"That's why he wanted to see me tonight," she raged, pacing the floor in fits and starts, throwing couch pillows against the walls. "He wasn't bringing a diamond ring for *me*, he was planning to break up with me!"

She wanted to call the man every evil name she could think of—just as her cell phone began to ring.

It was her mother.

She punched the button and stared at the screen. "Really, Mother, you're calling me now? It's midnight."

"Since when did you start calling me Mother? I've always been Mama."

Her mother's charming accent came through the line even though she'd spent the last thirty-five years of her life in California. Not too thick, but not too slight.

"Mama," Revé repeated. "It's very late, I'm in bed."

"No, you're not. I think you just got home, my darling girl."

"How would you know that?"

"Because your father just got a phone call from Mr. Dalton Bennett."

Revé groaned and flopped down on the couch. "Mother, I can explain."

"I can guess. Your dinner group watched the entire episode and, even though it was a bit shocking, Ms. Sampino explained that you were brilliant."

"For those watching the show, shocking is putting it mildly."

"I'm sure it's an exaggeration, dear. Why don't you call Warren and straighten all this out?"

Her mother, Anya Chatham, could never fathom anyone being dishonest, untrustworthy, or unfaithful. Despite a shrewd business sense and accounting brains coming out her ears, she liked to believe the best in everyone she knew. "There's nothing to straighten out. It's over."

"Surely it can't be that bad—"

"Worse. I have the whole thing on video. The diamond ring, the deep-throated kissing, the works." Revé's voice choked on the last words.

"Oh, darling, no," her mother said in a whisper. "I'm so sorry. I'm coming right over."

"Your chicken soup isn't going to help this one," Revé said, the words more bitter than she intended. After all, she knew her mother only wanted her daughter's happiness. The entire family had liked Warren and assumed their engagement was imminent.

Why wasn't she ever enough? Never good enough for the men she fell in love with. What was wrong with her? It was a bitter pill to swallow—again.

"Third times the charm, I think," Revé said. "I officially swear off men forever. God himself is going to have to come down and tell me who the right man is—

probably yell it in my ear—and then shine a halo of light on the guy."

"*Oh, honey,*" Her mother's voice was pained. "We're going to whisk you away to India and help you forget all about Warren and that horrible woman—"

"You're going to have to find some mind bleach. I think the sight of them together, and the huge diamond on her perfect, skinny finger is etched on my eyeballs forever."

"We need to find you a good man from India. I'm going to get out my address book and talk to all my friends and cousins—I'm sure there is a smart, nice-looking man close to your age—who has a doctorate degree in something—and a good family that would make the perfect husband."

"Stop," Revé ordered. The thought of her aunties—her mother had five sisters!—And all of those cousins made her sick to her stomach. She didn't want to face them. She couldn't. Tuesday's flight was coming much too fast.

"Why, what did I say?" her mother asked innocently.

"Come on, Mama, you know perfectly well what you're doing. And I'm not going to marry an Indian man. I was born here, in Los Angeles, I have nothing in common with potential husbands in India."

Her mother made a chirp of indignation. "Tsk, tsk. You're half Indian, remember? Half your family still lives there."

"How could I forget?" Revé said weakly, trying not to laugh while she wished she could get off the phone and cry instead.

But even though hot emotion burned behind her eyes, the tears weren't coming. Usually, she would be weeping with grief and hurt, crying for three days straight, but for some reason, all she wanted to do was smash Warren's crystal collection. And rear-end his pride and joy—that brand-new cherry red Ferrari—into a large, brick wall.

While she was at it, she'd rip out that woman's perfect blonde hair and magenta fingernails.

"You've gone awfully quiet, Revé. I can only imagine what you're thinking and feeling."

"I'm not sure you can, Mother," Revé said, biting her tongue as she tried not to smile at what she was *really* thinking. "I'm going to bed, I'm exhausted. I'll talk to you tomorrow."

"Are you packed yet?"

"No."

"That will take your mind off your troubles, sweetheart."

Revé grimaced. Actually, no, it wouldn't. Now she just had a whole new set of things to fret over, like all of her gossiping, non-stop talking relatives for the next two weeks. Without a doubt, her aunties had already spread the word of her horrific betrayal by Warren Dailey.

Midnight right now was just after lunch in New Delhi. Her aunts would be shopping and decorating and baking and cleaning house for the holidays. And talking. Endlessly talking, especially if her mother had already called them about her only daughter's fresh romantic woes.

Romantic woes were a topic of great delight to any female relative. Especially when that niece or cousin had suffered through three—*three* terrible breakups in the last several years.

They would assume Revé would be in mourning.

"Just don't put together a funeral dirge—or a wake—for my love life, okay?"

"Would my sisters and I ever do such a silly thing?" Her mother's tinkling laugh came through the phone.

Yes, they would, Revé thought. "Goodnight, Mama."

"Okay, tomorrow, no work. I will tell your father no work for you. Focus on packing. Many suitcases with clothes for every occasion and nights out and dancing and parties."

It was all Revé could do not to throw her phone across the room and stomp it into tiny little metal pieces.

There was no way she was packing to go to India. She was going to take her rebellion one step further. She was not going to India for the holidays at all.

She was going to stay right here in Los Angeles. Better yet, she'd go down to San Diego and get a beach house and drink all the margaritas she could swallow without getting sick. Which wasn't very many since she didn't actually drink.

Well, that plan wasn't going to work. Instead, Revé would find a beach and drink Coke—a twelve pack every day until she was sick and jittery with caffeine.

Rolling off the bed, she threw on some sweats and a hoodie, grabbed her wallet and keys and jogged down to the corner market, picking up a 2-liter bottle of Coke, a handful of candy bars and three microwave popcorn packets.

Back at her apartment, she settled under a pile of blankets with her snacks and a tall glass, Coke sizzling over the ice cubes while she brought up her all-time favorite movie, *The Princess Bride*. She needed to laugh, to be transported away from her own sorry life.

And she did, laughing hysterically at the bald and spitting know-it-all Vizzini who repeats "Inconceivable" until he keels over dead—and cheering for Inigo Montoya who finally enacts his revenge on the six-fingered man who killed his father. The reunion of Westley and Buttercup always made her choke up when he finally removes his mask and she sees the man she had thought was dead for four years.

By the end of the movie, Revé had eaten the Snickers bar, a big bowl of popcorn, and drunk most of the 2-liter soda. And this was after the fabulous dinner at The Markus.

"Okay, back to my regularly scheduled diet tomorrow," she said aloud, pulling the warm blanket up to her chin for the final climactic moment of the movie—her absolute all-time favorite last two minutes of any movie she had ever seen—when Westley kisses Buttercup.

The narrator said, *"Since the invention of the kiss, there have been five kisses that have been rated the most passionate, the most pure—this one left them all behind."*

A few tears leaked from Revé's eyes and she rewound the kiss three more times to watch Westley and Buttercups lips slowly come together in the perfect, passionate kiss, Westley's hand pressed against Buttercup's head and her luscious golden locks.

"Ack," she sighed savagely grabbing a tissue to dab at her eyes. "Darn you, movie—why do you have to torture me with a possibility that might never happen?"

If Revé was honest with herself, none of her long-time boyfriends, or fiancés, had ever kissed her in the way that Westley and Buttercup's passionate kiss was described.

"So why are you crying, you idiot?" she snapped at herself while she snapped off the kitchen lights and checked the alarm system.

It was three o'clock in the morning, and Revé was just feeling sorry for herself.

But would she ever meet a man that would give her the most passionate, the most pure and marvelous kiss of her life? That was the $25,000 dollar question. One that Revé was 100% certain that after tonight would never happen.

CHAPTER 4

*R*evé forgot to turn the sound off on her cell phone so when it rang the next morning before eight AM, she was so groggy she wasn't sure where she was, except in the middle of a dream where she was stuck in a cabin on the edge of a mountain, snowbound with no way out for six months.

"Maybe I do need a break from my life," she muttered, searching frantically for her phone, just to find it plugged into the wall next to her bed. "I was actually looking forward to not getting out of the imaginary cabin until the spring thaw—and now I'm talking to myself."

"Hey," Revé said hoarsely, seeing her best friend, Carmen Hurley's name on the screen. "Who wakes up this early on the weekend?"

"You sound terrible," Carmen said cheerfully.

"Gosh, thanks, I love you, too," Revé retorted. "I think it's the sleeping pill I took last night after eating myself silly over *The Princess Bride*. I feel like I've been drugged."

"That's because you *have* been drugged—a self-induced sugar coma. And why are you taking sleeping pills? That's not like you."

"Why you ask? His initials are Warren Dailey," Revé spit out. Just saying his name hurt her throat.

"Did you get your diamond ring last night?" Carmen squealed, obviously not tuning in to Revé's unfortunate mood.

There was a moment of silence while Revé hit the remote control of her T.V. to see if the world was still spinning.

"What a minute," Carmen said slowly. "You don't sound like a girl that just got engaged and had the night of her life."

"You're so astute, old roommate."

"*No.* What happened? Is Warren still alive? Or is he in a coma?"

"He's perfectly healthy and alive and blissfully-beyond-belief happy," Revé told her, unable to stop the bitterness from creeping into her voice.

"Spill it," Carmen said shortly, listening without uttering a single word while Revé told her the entire sordid story, except for appropriate groans and moans and shocked expletives.

"You have it on camera?" Carmen asked at the end. "Nice job getting blackmail if you need it."

"I'm done, Carmen. No more men. Ever. No more blind dates, double dates, online dating. I can't take it."

"Just because you met the last three jerks in the world of men doesn't mean they're all like that."

"The ones who aren't jerks are already married. Or widowed by the woman of their dreams who still wear their wedding ring and put their wife's picture under their pillows," Revé added with a snort of laughter.

"That laugh sounds pretty good." Carmen paused. "Are you okay, or should I come over with a rescue package and a plan to escape and go wild for the weekend? At least before you leave for your grandmother's house next week."

Revé's breath caught. A wild and crazy thought jumped into her brain. "Carmen," she said slowly. "What would you think about me *really* escaping? For real. Like, leave Los Angeles and all this insanity behind and come to your house in New Mexico for Christmas. . .um, is it terrible if I invite myself? Or were you hinting, ha-ha?"

Carmen gasped. "Revé, are you serious? I'd *love* to have you visit me in New Mexico! You've never been here! I've always wanted to show off my world, but I know your family obligations are like, written in stone."

"Well, the stone contract *has* been cracking. At least on my end. Carmen, I just don't think I can face all the questions and sorrowful looks of sympathy between my aunts and cousins next week. Especially the way Warren humiliated me by proposing to some strange woman he's been having an affair with and then making out at their dinner table! Oh, my cousins will have a *great* time with all that juicy stuff!"

"Spend Christmas with me!" Carmen urged. "It's a brilliant idea. You're thirty-four years old. You run a billionaire dollar company with your father—you can go have a vacation by yourself if you want to!"

Revé bit at her lips. "Well, I have to admit that the smog of Los Angeles has been getting to me and I've been craving a white Christmas—which I have never, ever had, by the way! I want to chop down a Christmas tree and drink hot cocoa by the fire and snuggle up under a blanket with a movie. I've lived a sheltered life in Southern California, haven't I?" she added with a small, pathetic laugh.

"Those are my New Mexico Christmas traditions, plus a whole lot more, girl! When can you get here?"

"I have to check flights—and break it to my folks. I wonder if I could just leave a note."

"I'll call them and tell them for you!"

Revé burst into giggles, the hard knot in her throat disappearing the longer she talked to her old friend. "You're brave, Carmen. No . . . I'll do the dirty work of reneging on my family holiday obligations, although I'll probably hear the shrieks and screams all the way across the ocean."

"Tell your family that you're wasting away from tuberculosis or something."

"That only happened in the opera *La Boheme*."

"Make up a story about running off with some guy you met in the bar last night."

"You're terrible!" Revé spluttered. "They'd never believe that about me."

Her friend's voice turned mischievous. "I'll bet they'd be happy, actually!"

Revé rolled out of bed she was laughing so hard. "Oh, gosh, you're right. They'd all love to come to America for a wedding—mine! I don't think the man I marry matters, just the wedding! The biggest, flashiest, most expensive wedding ever."

"Okay, go wipe your eyes and get dressed. I'm calling the airlines right now. Be ready to receive your e-ticket in 15 minutes."

"Aye, aye, Miss Hurley. Alexa is going to die when she hears about what I'm doing."

"Who's that? One of your cousins?"

"No, my assistant at work. She's been telling me to rebel for years now."

"She sounds like my kind of friend," Carmen said gaily. "Ta-ta for now! Talk soon!"

CHAPTER 5

Revé's head was spinning when she boarded the plane three days later for Albuquerque, New Mexico. She swore it felt like she was headed to a foreign country, although it was only two states away.

"Do you need your international passport?" Her mother had asked after Revé broke the news and the wailing finally ceased.

"Nope. It turns out New Mexico is actually part of the United States! How about that?"

When she told Carmen what her mother had said, her friend laughed hysterically. "Hey, we have a zip code, too. We've been a regular state for well over a hundred years. Don't be a silly East Coast girl and insist there's nothing between Arizona and Texas—it's a big beautiful state with mountains and the Rio Grande and cotton-woods and Native American pueblos and red chile's hanging on the porches, and tamales and scrumptious sopapillas hot out of the deep fryer with honey for Christmas Eve dinner. And yes, half the state does speak Spanish."

"I'm from California, not the East Coast," Revé retorted, trying not to laugh in return.

"Practically the same thing, honey," Carmen said drily.

Of course, the conversations with her parents and her brother wasn't nearly as easy. Her mother was *shocked* that Revé was backing out of the annual family trip to her hometown and all the extended family. Didn't she understand that it was *a tradition*!

As if their yearly trip to India was like a religious pilgrimage and Revé was committing a sin.

"Mama," she said repeatedly, trying to explain. "I just can't go this year. I'm too emotionally distraught."

"You *sound* perfectly fine to me," Anya Chatham accused suspiciously.

"I cry every night into my pillow," Revé lied, crossing her fingers behind her back. She was disappointing her mother, but when she thought about boarding that plane and trying not to get aggravated by her well-meaning, but often nosey family, she just couldn't bring herself to go.

By the morning of the second day, she was tired of being outraged by Warren. She refused to be a victim of a man who was apparently a selfish, unfeeling jerk.

She'd actually dodged a bullet, right? Why weep over someone who had treated her in such a despicable manner?

But deep in her heart, Revé wanted a family of her own. Children to tuck into bed each night, and hold their hand when it was time to face the scary dentist.

She wanted it all—and that dream seemed elusive most of the time. Then Revé's father called upon his return from San Francisco.

"Hey, Daddy, how was the trip?"

"Rainy. Wet. Windy. The usual."

"But it's such a pretty city."

"Downtown was decorated very nice, and we tried a new restaurant in Chinatown that was superb."

"I get to go with you next time, okay? I'll plan the itinerary for all the fun we'll have after we complete our business."

"Quit stalling, my darling girl," he told her in his deep voice. "So it's over with Warren?"

"Completely. Irrevocably."

"Can't say I'm sad to hear it."

"What?" Revé was shocked.

"Something about that man always rubbed me the wrong way."

"Guess I'm terrible at picking men. Every time I think it's the one, he's NOT – in a big way!"

"You'll know when you find the right man. The one you're meant to be with."

"You're such a romantic, Daddy."

"I want what's best for you." He paused as if choosing his words carefully. "Your mother is pretty upset about you canceling the trip. It'll be the first time in your life that we go without you—that we're not together during the holidays."

"I only canceled *me*. You guys go—and have a blast. I get to go somewhere new and exotic, too, and I haven't seen Carmen in ages."

"Did I ever tell you that your mother and I went through New Mexico on our honeymoon. We were fresh out of college, driving an old '68 Chevy cross-country to get to Columbia for grad school. Loved it. Its nickname is the Land of Enchantment, and it was. There's a powerful ancient spirit about that state. Lots of history and great, down-to-earth people. You'll love the food, too, my spicy Indian-food loving daughter."

"It sounds wonderful. I need a change of scenery, and it will be my first white Christmas."

"Well, that settles it. Snow boots and mittens for you this winter. I'll take care of things with your mother— and give your love to your granny for you. Take pictures, freeze your toes, and go for a hike in the hills of Taos."

"I promise. And please tell granny that I'll visit her in the spring before it gets too hot.

"Keep in touch, sweetheart—and fly straight back

home if you need anything," he added with a fatherly growl.

The flight was only two hours but when Revé saw Carmen standing at the bottom of the escalator near baggage claim, she launched into her arms.

"It's been way too long," Revé said. "You look wonderful, although you're bundled up like a snowman—snow-woman, I mean!"

"Hope you packed a big jacket and muffler, girl," Carmen said. "Your southern California is showing."

"And how's that?" Revé said, sticking a hand on her hip.

"For one thing, you have much better clothing stores there—and you have an excellent haircut."

"Thanks, but I'm here to play in the snow, sit by the fire, sleep late, and eat oodles of Christmas cookies."

Carmen linked arms with her, and they headed down to the baggage area. Albuquerque International airport was just one single terminal, but decorated with Native American artwork and thick notched beams called vigas running across the three-story high ceilings.

"I already feel like I've been transported to a different world," Revé noted. "I love the unique Southwestern decor."

"Just you wait," Carmen teased. "Did you like the green chile I sent you?"

"Loved it. Yummy and hot, just like my granny's cooking."

"Here in New Mexico, we eat it with practically every dish so get your taste buds ready. Now how long are you staying?"

"As long as you'll have me, but at least a week?"

"Perhaps you didn't notice, but I left your airline ticket open-ended," Carmen said with a wink.

"You'll get sick of me before too long."

"Never. It's been years since we had a girl's weekend. Please stay two weeks – a month if you need it! Warren sounds like a real piece of work—I was going to say a nasty word, but I'll be a good girl."

"Wanna see the video I have of him proposing to another woman in the restaurant?"

"You still have it? I'm *dying* to see it. And then we'll have a ceremonially purging and burn him at the stake—in my backyard!"

Revé nearly fell over with laughter. "That's not a bad idea."

"When Rob and I separated, I burned all of our personal mushy stuff. I couldn't handle it—not when he moved in with some chick from work."

"I'm so sorry you went through all that," Revé said, empathy welling inside her chest. "That's worse than anything I've endured."

"It's been two years, so I'm doing better, but I'm so glad you're here at last. We can do all sorts of girl things and stay up all night talking. Thanks for sacrificing your family to hang with me."

"You're saving *me* from two weeks of awkward whispers and gossip. Oh, here's my luggage." Revé pulled her two suitcases off the carousel.

Carmen grabbed one of the rolling bags. "I'm glad you took a morning flight so you can see the scenery on our two-hour drive north to Taos while it's still daylight."

After piling the luggage into the trunk, Carmen started the engine of her Prius and soon they were headed north on the interstate which would take them to Santa Fe until they made a northeastern turn to the idyllic town of Taos nestled in the mountains.

"The scenery is spectacular," Revé said, leaning forward to gaze through the windshield a dozen times over. "What are these mountains called? They just keep tumbling over each other in so many colors."

"It's the Sangre de Cristo range—Blood of Christ it means in Spanish. Some of the peaks are more than thirteen thousand feet. We have four ski resorts nearby. *Angel Fire, Taos Ski Resort. Red River* and *Sipapu* Ski Resort. *Sipapu* is a Native American word that means the place of origin where the people originally emerged into this world."

"I love that. Having a special word for where you came from."

"Did I tell you that my parents went up to Colorado to ski for the next week before Christmas actually hits?"

"How could they be bored with the usual resorts right in their backyard?" Revé asked.

"Ha! They're passionate about their skiing, so you nailed it. Plus, my mother has two sisters in Colorado Springs that they're going to spend the holidays with—which meant I could invite you and we can have the entire house to ourselves."

"Sounds fantastic," Revé said, leaning back into her bucket seat and feeling more relaxed than she had in weeks and weeks. "Just don't make me snow ski—I'll fall flat on my face."

"We must remedy that! I'll make you run the bunny hill," Carmen threatened with an arch of her eyebrow.

"Does this mean you're still living with your folks?"

"Well, yes and no. Rob and I split everything 50/50 when the divorce finalized," Carmen said in a quieter voice. "I moved back in with my parents to save money, but rents and home prices are so expensive I couldn't afford my own place, and I didn't want roommates—not at *our* age, so my dad had a little cottage built for me on the property. They have five acres so it's quiet and gorgeous. And I get my privacy and personal space."

"Sounds perfect. Tell me all about the amazing things to do in Taos for Christmas! Besides popcorn and movies and eating amazing Mexican food, that is?"

"I made a list. First we'll chop down our very own Christmas tree in the pine forest. Then decorate it with lights and the boxes and boxes of ornaments from

Mom's storage shed. We'll drive around to see amazing Christmas lights. Eat dinner at the town square. Listen to the nightly music at the plaza. Watch *It's a Wonderful Life* and *Rudolph the Red-Nosed Reindeer—*"

"You mean the original version with the abominable snowman?"

"None other!" Carmen shot back with a big grin. "Then we'll decorate sugar cookies—and eat until we're stuffed silly. Oh, and I'll teach you how to make tamales —it's a Christmas Eve tradition. If we're lucky, we'll get carolers roaming the neighborhood one night."

"Sounds perfect," Revé said as they turned off the main road and headed into the hills where ranch homes and adobe flat-roofed houses sat nestled off winding lanes and narrow roads. Scrub brush and pinon trees dotted the rocky hillsides.

The setting of Taos was like something out of an old western movie—with unique dashes of style and charm.

Earlier they had passed the Pueblo of Taos, the ancient Native American village, lights strung along the cottonwoods, hammered tin lanterns with pretty patterns hanging from the brown adobe buildings.

"We're going to take the tour of the pueblo one day and walk by the river," Carmen told her, turning up the side of a steep hill to head to the home she had grown up in.

"Where are the Los Alamos laboratories?" Revé

asked, remembering that Carmen's father had worked there for decades before retiring.

"A good hour's drive, but he loved living in Taos too much to move closer. It's a unique city in the pine forest, and the entire city is built on several flat rugged canyons all parallel to each other. Quite picturesque. It was called the secret city during World War II."

"There's so much to see and do I think I'd better stay a month," Revé said. "And there's still Santa Fe and Albuquerque's Old Town to tour."

"Please do stay if you can spare the time!" Carmen lifted her eyebrows at the temptation of playing hooky from their jobs—at the very same moment a black monster truck careened around a sharp curve in the road heading straight for them.

Revé yelped as Carmen jerked the wheel to avoid a collision, but the tires slipped and slid on the soft gravel, causing their vehicle to fishtail dangerously.

Even worse, on the passenger side where Revé sat, the steep ravine fell straight down to a desert floor she couldn't even see the bottom of.

If Revé shifted her weight even an inch, the Prius would teeter off the edge of the cliff and they would fall to their deaths.

CHAPTER 6

"We're going over the edge!" Revé screamed, watching her life flash before her eyes.

The car skidded to a stop and Carmen jerked at the emergency brake to hold the car in place, letting out a shaky breath.

The oncoming truck roared to a stop as well, sending up a cloud of dust in the bright afternoon sun, blinding Revé through the windshield.

Carmen slammed a fist against the steering wheel, turning off the engine. "Darn that Logan!" she muttered savagely.

"Who's Logan?" Revé asked, leaning toward her friend as if that would keep the car from tipping over the edge of the cliff where they would be dashed against the boulders lying below them about five hundred feet.

"The view down there is absolutely *frightening*. Will the car slip over the edge?"

"No, oh no! I'm sorry, Revé. We're further from the edge than it looks, but it *is* nerve-racking all the same."

"Who's Logan?" Revé asked again, thinking that person had the answer to their predicament, although she had no idea how. "Is he your mechanic?"

"I wish," Carmen said with a touch of irony. "Nope, *that* hunk of a male specimen in the truck is Logan Redmond. My *neighbor.*"

Revé stared through the windshield as the dust cleared. A tall, broad man exited his rumbling diesel truck, its back end filled to the gills with—well, something since there was a tarp tied down over the massive load he was carrying.

It was a chilly thirty-nine degrees by Carmen's car thermometer, but Logan Redmond wasn't wearing a coat, as if the cold had no effect on him. His chest and arms were bulky with muscles under the long-sleeved forest green Henley shirt he was wearing with his black jeans and cowboy boots.

Revé wasn't sure she'd ever seen such a sculpted, athletic man in her life—besides television or models on the grocery store magazine rack. She couldn't stop herself from staring until her eyes bulged. Taking a gulp, she finally eased against her seat and tried to release her death grip on the dashboard.

"You okay?" Carmen asked. "You've gone really pale."

"Um, yeah." Revé blinked and pressed a hand to her heart that was thudding against her ribs. "Good thing it's not dark or we might have gone over the cliff, right?"

Carmen shook her head. "I know it's a little scary, but probably not. Actually, I'd have seen Logan's headlights sooner if it was darker. Despite the narrow, rocky roads, we've never had an accident along here, even though I've lived here since I was a kid."

Still staring through the windshield, Revé noted that when Logan Redmond took off his cowboy hat, he boasted a full head of dirty blond shaggy hair that grazed his ears.

A pair of deep blue eyes literally caused her to stop breathing for a moment, including the week-old beard she found herself wanting to run her fingers down to see if it was as soft as it looked from this angle.

Carmen caught Revé's ogling and gave a twittering laugh. "Yeah, good old Logan is one gorgeous dude."

"Is he a cowboy?" Revé asked, suddenly wondering if Carmen was dating the man. A twinge of disappointment went through her, but she shook it off. How silly. He was just another nice-looking man.

"Not exactly. He doesn't manage a personal ranch and he only owns two horses for riding around the local trails."

"Oh," Revé said, her voice trailing off. "Just two horses. That's more than most people I know. But how many people actually round up cattle anymore, right?"

"You'd be surprised, actually," Carmen told her. "New Mexico has a lot of cattle ranches."

Cautiously, Revé peered through her side window at the sheer cliff drop below. "Um, could we please move a little closer to the middle of the road?"

"We're already in the middle of the road. One of us—me or Logan—is going to have to back up to let the other pass."

"What?" Revé didn't like the sound of that. "Wouldn't backing up be too dangerous?"

Carmen pulled open her door and slid out onto the gravel. "Hey, dude," she called out. "Back up. It's your turn."

"My turn?" Logan gave a deep, throaty laugh and the sound made Revé shiver with the sensuous sound.

Good grief, her entire body was on fire. "Stop it," she ordered under her breath, shaking off the goosebumps that had broken out along her neck and arms.

"It's your turn this time, Missy," Logan teased Carmen, the grin on his face spreading to reveal the brightest white teeth. The grin reminded Revé so much of Westley from *The Princess Bride* that she had to blink away the illusion. "I keep a log of turns, and I backed up the last three times."

"You are such a liar," Carmen shot back, hands on her hips. "You may have your big fat intimidating truck, but my Prius is much more delicate so haul your backside out of my way."

Slowly, Revé slid her own backside over the gear shift to get out of the car. If she sat there any longer she'd get so dizzy, she'd end up flinging herself off the side of the mountain.

Inch by inch, she finally plopped herself in the driver's seat, thinking how stupid she was to be such a ninny about the narrow road. After all, Carmen had driven it every single day for decades.

"Your friend's about to put that sissy car into reverse and leave you stranded," Logan told Carmen, his eyes latching onto Revé's face as she slid out of the vehicle, her legs wobbly.

"Ha! My car gets fifty miles to the gallon compared to the twelve you get in that hunk of junk."

Even though she was finally standing upright on the dirt road, Revé continued to hang onto the car door with both hands.

The diesel engine was making a considerable racket, so everyone was shouting to be heard, which Revé found very amusing. Carmen and Logan were arguing like they were teenagers. From their tones and saucy stances, she was getting the feeling that they did this all the time.

"How long have you two known each other?" she asked, stepping forward.

"Since Kindergarten," Carmen said over her shoulder. "Logan used to pull my braids until I beat him at the

100-yard dash—before he suddenly shot up to six feet the following year."

"He made six feet tall by first grade? That's quite a feat," Revé said without cracking a smile.

Carmen burst out giggling. "You always could do dead-pan well, Revé. I stopped wearing braids by fifth grade, but we were always competing in sports and grades. It's too bad," she added, lowering her voice. "Because he's one of the best-looking men I've ever met, and yet, we're like buddies, no romance at all."

Revé peered at her, curious. "Do you wish it was different?"

Carmen shrugged with a shake of her head. "Nope. Logan is a good guy and always has my back, but if we were to start dating, it would be like dating my brother. Although I've always wondered if he's a good kisser. I'll have to leave that to someone else to find out."

Throwing Revé a quick wink, she strode forward to inspect the front of her vehicle.

Revé followed, curious as to just how close to the edge they were. "Oh," she said. "You're right. We're about five feet from the edge. Even so, five feet on the edge of a deadly drop-off is too close for comfort for this city girl."

The next moment, Logan was beside her, gazing into Revé's face, his eyes taking her in, all of her, as if puzzling her out. She sucked in a quick breath and stepped back, trying to retain a measure of calm coolness and not the fear from two minutes earlier.

"Sorry for scaring you girls," Logan told Revé. "You chose the wrong best friend today."

"It appears I did—and the wrong neighbor to collide with," Revé added tartly. "That was some crazy fast driving."

"I'm sorry," he said again. "I don't usually meet someone on this stretch in the middle of the day, let alone Carmen. I forgot she was heading to the airport to pick someone up. You must be the someone." He gave her a wide, slow smile and held out his hand in greeting.

Revé stared down at his large, beautiful hand. Rugged, but no gnarly knuckles. Not too slender, not too thick, just really masculine and attractive.

She gave it a quick shake and fought the reaction she was having at the warmth and strength in that perfect, manly hand. "I'm going to take the opportunity to stay mad at you for a little longer. My heart is still about to jump out of my chest."

He gave a half bow. "Didn't mean to give you a heart attack, but please believe me when I say that you weren't in mortal danger."

Revé gave him a sideways impertinent glare. "Mortal danger is debatable. I'll decide that for myself."

"I didn't mean to scare the life out of you," he added, his voice pleasant and penitent. "I'm Logan Redmond, by the way. Neighbor, instigator of crazy, part cowboy, part city boy, and often a pain in the you-know-what."

"Is that guy bothering you?" Carmen called out after inspecting the width of the road.

"Not too much," Revé shot back, jumping into the teasing with both feet. "But I think he's harmless."

"Most of the time," Carmen added.

"Do you want to introduce me to your friend, *neighbor*?" Logan pointedly asked Carmen.

"This is my amazing, wonderful, and gorgeous friend from long-ago. College to be precise. Revé Chatham."

Logan tipped his cowboy hat back from his forehead, deepening his gaze on her face until Revé's skin prickled and she was sure her neck was turning a bright red. "Nice to meet you, Revé. Is that French?"

She nodded. "My mother is from India, but she lived in France during her teen years while her father was an ambassador there. The name means "dream.""

"Ooh, I love that," Carmen said, interrupting Revé's locked gaze on her rogue neighbor. "I don't think you ever told me that."

"Dream is a beautiful name for a beautiful woman," Logan said, his eyes still on Revé's face.

"Oh, please," Carmen said with a snort, sashaying closer. "You're such a flirt."

Logan opened his mouth in surprise and shook his head vigorously.

Revé jumped in to the conversation's patter. "Don't

say things you don't mean just to score points with your neighbor's friend."

"I always say what I mean," he told her, lowering his voice and giving her a clear-eyed expression. "I'm truthful and sincere—and if you need anything while you're in Taos for the holidays, please call. I can fix anything, make emergency calls, break a horse, haul logs, chop firewood, you name it."

"You run women off the road quite well, too," Revé threw back. He really had given her a good scare, and she wanted him to know it.

"Point taken, and I'll apologize to my dying day. The county needs to regrade this blind curve."

"Why wait for the county?" Revé challenged. "If you're so handy with everything, I'm sure you can fix it."

"I'll get me a tractor first thing in the morning," Logan said, boyishly grinning.

A laugh rose up Revé's throat, certain he was putting on the cowboy bad grammar just for her. "Where are you going to find a tractor by tomorrow morning?"

"He can get his hands on anything," Carmen spoke up. "He owns the rental place in town. Household items, appliances, farm equipment. Anything."

"And I know how to use them," Logan added.

"Don't get too cocky," Carmen warned. "Now back up so we can pass. Revé's been traveling since before dawn, and I want to take her on a tour of Taos before it's dark."

"Dark is the best time of the day. At least during the Christmas season." Logan gave a smile and Revé couldn't help zeroing in on his impeccably perfect mouth. "Taos goes all out for Christmas."

"That's why I came. And for the snow. Although it's colder than I expected."

"Hey, it's a balmy, sunny December 18th. Just wait until we go below zero in January."

"By then I'll be back home in Los Angeles," Revé said, her own mouth lifting into a smile. "Sunbathing."

"That's a sight worth going to smoggy Los Angeles for," he said in a low voice.

Carmen rolled her eyes and whacked him on the arm. "Oh my gosh, cut it out, Logan. Let Revé unpack before you overwhelm her with your over-the-top small-town charm."

"But Los Angeles also has Disneyland," Logan added. "I love Pirates of the Caribbean."

"You're impossible, Mr. Redmond," Carmen said with a sigh before turning to Revé to explain. "Logan's annual family vacation was driving the family mini-van to the Happiest Place on Earth, and he still likes to go every other year."

"I like Disneyland, too," Revé admitted. "And California Adventure. And Universal Studios. I have an annual pass."

Logan whistled. "Now that's worth its weight in gold. See you around, Revé," he said, tipping his cowboy hat before striding back to his truck. Jumping into the cab, he revved the loud engine, put it in reverse and backed up about a hundred feet to give them space to get around his vehicle.

"This is our chance, Revé!" Carmen yelled. "Slide in—no my side—I don't trust you not to fall over the edge."

"I don't trust me either, Revé admitted, her skin prickling when she glanced at the steep ravine again while sliding through the driver's side back to her own passenger seat. "That drop scares the heck out of me."

"You already sound like a small-town girl. That didn't take long. Let's get some lunch, and I'll let you unpack—and then we'll make our list of devious, wonderful holiday plans."

CHAPTER 7

The Hurley home was spectacular. Carmen parked in the curving drive that led to beautifully laid brick pathways that ended at double French doors with beveled glass windows.

Once inside, the foyer opened into a huge great room with twenty feet high ceilings decorated by rugged viga beams.

An adobe fireplace was set into the wall with blood-red tiles, and a seating area with pillows for lounging beside groupings of comfy furniture and lamps.

The rooms were large and spacious with big picture windows overlooking the front and back gardens with sloping hills and sagebrush and pine trees.

"It's absolutely lovely!" Revé exclaimed as Carmen took her on a tour. "I love all the windows and the sun streaming in. And your kitchen is enormous! Do you ever get lost in here?"

"Oh, yeah, all the time," Carmen said with a serious face while she made sandwiches and set out chips and green chile dip for snacking.

"Yuuummy," Revé said with delight.

"Mom left all kinds of frozen meals in the freezer, including the deep freeze in the garage packed with all the holiday food and trimmings. I swear she grocery shopped for two days straight."

"How thoughtful of her! I wish they could have been here, too. I only remember meeting them at our college parent weekend many years ago."

"Let's make a list of things we want to do," Carmen said, lounging in one of the armchairs with a pad and pen. "The town square and Christmas lights are a must. A tour of the Taos Pueblo, too. Taking goodies to the neighbors—mom's orders. Are you up for a hike in the hills? The rattlesnakes are hibernating."

"Rattlesnakes?" Revé echoed.

"We won't see a single snake, I promise."

"It's not too cold for hiking?"

"We'll go in the afternoon on a sunny day and bundle up good." Carmen consulted her calendar. "We have a New Year's Eve dinner and party to go to with friends from my job. I *may* want to introduce you to a certain man that might be a good match, but I have to think about it still."

"Don't tease me!" Revé said, her thoughts immediately steering toward Logan Redmond and his devastatingly perfect physique and blue eyes. For all her annoyance and fright, he had a playful, good-hearted nature about him and perfectly gorgeous eyes.

When she looked up again, Carmen was gazing at her, an eyebrow raised. "Were you daydreaming about something in particular just now?"

"No," Revé said, widening her eyes. "Maybe my six-a.m. flight just smacked me in the face."

"I'm all for naps, but I need to go dig up our permit so we can go up into the hill to cut down our Christmas tree."

"We're really going to cut our own tree?" Revé had no idea what that was like. Her mother always had fancy, fake trees with thousands of lights and perfectly matched ornaments—a different theme each year. There was an entire storage shed devoted just to Christmas decorations.

"It's an adventure. I'll grab an extra big jacket for you. The only problem is, I need to find someone with a truck that's willing to haul it home for us—or let us borrow a truck. Dad took his up to Colorado, or I'd grab his keys."

"You need to find someone with a truck?" Revé repeated, leaning forward with a chortle of laughter. "I don't live here, and yet I know someone who owns one who's initials are L.R."

Carmen brushed the suggestion aside. "I know you're talking about Logan, but after today I'm annoyed with him, and I'm sure you don't want to spend another minute with the man."

Casually, Revé sat back, curling her legs underneath her while watching gray clouds rolling across the plate glass windows. "Oh, yeah," she said. "Why would we want to spend time with Logan?"

Except she was actually curious, and she did want to see him again despite his annoyingly loud truck. She had a sudden image of her fingers entwined with Logan's while they hiked a narrow canyon road to find the perfect Christmas tree.

When she realized what she was thinking about, Revé inwardly berated herself. What an idiot she was! There was no way in the world she was going to start up any sort of dating relationship, *or* even a friendship, with another man. It hadn't even been a week since Warren's betrayal.

And yet, she never even *thought* about Warren anymore. It was as if he'd never existed. After his betrayal it had become painfully obvious that Warren was a nondescript, boring man—except for his secret double love life. Who would have ever thought the guy would do something like that?

"Let me think about the truck issue," Carmen said, bringing Revé back to the present. She tapped the pen against her lips thoughtfully. "I'll get us a truck while you finish unpacking and take a nap. Perhaps we can get the tree tomorrow after breakfast. That way we can get it set up and decorated by dinner time."

"Sounds excellent, Revé said, yawning despite her efforts to prop her eyelids open.

Later, after she was settled into the lovely guest room with its own bathroom and thick towels hanging on a heated towel rack, she took a power nap before waking up to Carmen's homemade enchiladas and red chile sauce. It was covered in layers of decadent melted Colby and cheddar cheese.

"I swear this is better than any Mexican restaurant I've ever been to," Revé told her, dishing up a second helping.

"My mom's a great cook. She used to work in a restaurant way back when Mike and I were little kids while my dad was finishing his Ph.D. in Physics."

"You have cool parents," Revé said with a grin. "So do I, whenever they're home."

"Your life has really changed a lot in the last decade, hasn't it?"

"The pharmaceutical labs and company has been around for twenty years, but yeah, ten years ago when we had that successful diabetic testing product come onto the market, things really took off. Now, with this effective new cancer drug, we've exploded." Revé grew thoughtful. "My parents are gone a lot visiting hospitals and clinics and the three laboratories around the country, so I miss them. And my own job intensified, but it feels completely and utterly bizarre that I'm going to inherit a billion-dollar company."

"You're already part of it. So, you guys all swimming in the green stuff?"

Revé laughed out loud. "Yeah, right. The expenses and insurance alone would support an apartment building of families."

"Sorry, I can't help but be curious," Carmen said. "My own parents have lived a comfortable life in our little town, but your life has to be beyond astonishing these days."

A little embarrassed, Revé nodded. "I try not to think about it—or talk about it—but it's amazing what the company has managed to accomplish. It's truly bizarre though to call myself a billionaire, even though my dad stuffed my 401K and IRA accounts to the max. I *feel* exactly the same. Job stress, men problems, extended family that can drive me up a wall, envious of my brother with five darling kids and a perfect wife."

Carmen hugged one of the throw pillows to her chest. "You'll find the perfect man, I know he's out there somewhere—for both of us. Meanwhile, let's go down to the town plaza and see the lights. I hear there's a band playing under the gazebo tonight."

"Sounds perfect," Revé jumped up to pull on thick socks and grab her jacket and muffler, checking her makeup and hair in the mirror. Just in case. "Gosh, I'm an idiot. I'm not here to find a man, but maybe I do need to get out of Southern California more."

When they slid into the Prius and began the winding drive into town, Carmen said, "I thought it would be fun to take a picnic with us tomorrow for our tree-cutting adventure. We can pack sandwiches and chips and sodas."

"That sounds great. Just remind me to bring a knitted hat and mittens tomorrow!"

Downtown Taos was quaint and charming, a cozy village with narrow roads that wound around the low hills. Adobe-style antique stores, cafes, and gift shops surrounded the brick and stone center plaza with patches of grass and a center dais where a country-style four-person band played Christmas melodies with enthusiasm.

Along one side of the square of shops was the luxurious Hotel La Fonda, its lights lit up like a beacon. Taos had gone all out on Christmas decorations. The giant cottonwood trees had been lit with sparkly lights wrapped around the wide trunks and followed all the way up the limbs. The pathways were outlined with lights, too, and there was a Nutcracker display with lit up soldiers and a dancing ballerina.

In the very center of the plaza close to where the band had just started playing, "Santa Claus is Coming to Town", an enormous forty-foot-tall tree was a myriad of lights reaching into the dusky sky.

A few luminarias—brown paper bags filled with two inches of sand where a votive candle had been lit—lined the front windows of several of the shops, glowing a dusky yellow color in the dark night.

"We'll come back on Christmas Eve", Carmen said. "On that night, the entire plaza lays out thousands of luminarias all along the walkways and trees. It will literally take your breath away."

"That sounds amazing."

"I bought the supplies to make our own, too. All the paper bags and candles. About a hundred of them to put around the front of the house, up the driveway, and along the flower beds. We set them out before dusk on Christmas Eve afternoon. All the houses on our hillside put up luminarias, and it's just the prettiest sight you'll ever see on Christmas Eve. I just love that tradition."

"What does it mean?" Revé asked. "How did it get started?"

"I think it began hundreds of years ago. Luminarias show the Christ Child the way to your house so He can visit your family and bring His spirit to bless your family with His Everlasting Peace."

"What a lovely idea," Revé said softly, lifting her face to the cold air to gaze at the lights and the enormous cottonwood trees shining with red and green and gold lights.

"They're also called *farolitos,*" Carmen said. "Original luminarias were more like small bonfires, but the *farolitos* were created in colorful wrapping paper when families began making the smaller version for their homes."

A feeling of peace rose in Revé's entire being. "Being here in the mountains feels so far from the hustle and bustle in the big cities where it's all about the commercial aspect of the holiday. I love going back to the original traditions and meaning of Christmas. Now I'm feeling a little guilty about not going to New Delhi. I've deserted my family on the most important family holiday of the year."

"*You're* my family this year, Revé," Carmen said as they strolled the plaza. "Otherwise I'd be alone."

Revé gave her friend a tender look. "That's true. I'm glad I'm here with you, too."

"Let's go in here and get a basket of sopapillas," Carmen suggested. "We'll make them on Christmas Eve, too, so you might get sick of them, but they're so yummy, I doubt it," she added.

When Revé sank her teeth into the honey drizzled sopapilla, which turned out to be a fried, puffy piece of pastry, she moaned with pleasure. "This is fantastic. They remind me of *beignets* in New Orleans, except I think they're even more delicious. And this little café is charming."

She gazed at the local art hanging on the walls, and the bustling waitresses in colorful blouses. Through the window where their table sat, she could hear the band in the square now playing *I'm Dreaming of a White Christmas*, followed by *Jingle Bells*. A group of people stopped to sing with them.

"Having a third one," Revé announced, picking up the honey jar to adorn the hollow donut-like delicacy with a big, fat glob. "You'd think I never had dinner."

"The cold air and walking always gives me an appetite, too," Carmen agreed with a grin.

"Did you two beautiful women save me a sopapilla?" a male voice said behind Revé. She turned with a start, her eyes rising to see Logan Redmond standing not a foot away.

CHAPTER 8

"*Y*ou mean one of these incredible delicacies?" Carmen asked, picking up the basket and holding it to her chest. Both Logan and Revé laughed at her antics. "Nothin' doin'. Get your own basket, buddy."

"I already ordered one," Logan said, "But every table is packed."

"Well, slide in here with us, I guess," Carmen said in a teasing tone. "We have the Christmas spirit, don't we, Revé?"

"Um, of course." Revé paused for a split second, and suddenly realized that Carmen wasn't sliding over to make room on her bench seat for Logan. She widened her eyes to glare at her friend, scooting closer to the window to make room for the tall, broad-shouldered man.

His arm brushed against hers, and she shivered despite the roaring fire in the main room that made the café toasty warm.

She'd pulled her jacket off earlier, and now his shoulder met hers briefly. She bit at her lips, overcome for a moment by his nearness. His presence was unexpected, and now she sat up straight, wondering if her hair was a rat's mess after wearing the knitted hat pulled over her head while they'd walked the plaza.

"How do you like Taos so far, Revé?" Logan asked, his voice softening, almost melodic when he spoke her name. "And sopapillas?"

"Taos is gorgeous, and sopapillas are my new favorite food—after Carmen's out-of-this-world enchiladas, of course."

"You don't have to butter me up, Revé."

"I only speak the truth," she told Carmen. "I think every meal is going to be a new adventure over the next two weeks—and every single one a new favorite."

"Ah," Logan said. "Then you're here for more than a long weekend, Revé."

She nodded, hyper aware of his delicious masculine scent. "Our offices are closed until after New Year's, but I took some vacation time to come early."

Carmen chimed in. "Revé hasn't had a decent vacation away from her power-house office in over a year so she told her family she was deserting them and hopped on a plane."

"Well, it wasn't *exactly* like that," Revé protested.

"What *is* your family doing without you?" Logan asked, sincere curiosity on his face. "And when we're talking family, do you mean a husband and kids?"

"Oh, no," Revé laughed. "I'm not married."

Revé noticed that Logan's eyes flicked to her left hand which was bare of any wedding rings.

"Carmen is referring to my parents and brother—who does have five children—and all of my mother's extended family in India," Revé explained.

"That's quite a trip to cancel," Logan noted.

"We've traveled to New Delhi every year since I was a toddler. It was time to play hooky—for a variety of reasons," Revé added slowly.

Logan shifted in his seat to look at her more directly. He gave her a devastating smile that melted her insides. "I have a feeling your 'reasons' part is confidential."

"Your intuition serves you well," Revé said primly, hoping he wasn't going to ask further questions. She took a sip of her ice water, trying to hide the vibes zinging between them.

Logan's penetrating eyes seemed to burn her skin, making her hot all the way to the core of her insides. It was the strangest sensation, something she had never felt before, especially with a man she had barely met.

His presence was magnetic as if he were a famous actor or a wealthy tycoon—and yet that didn't even come close. Logan seemed comfortable in his own skin.

Confident without being arrogant. He had a lovely voice and kind eyes without being weak. Instead, just the opposite.

A true warmth radiated from him, and Revé feared that if he touched her, she would burn with a thousand volts of electricity.

Each of her senses was on high alert as if one wrong move would shatter her—or she'd fall madly, instantly in love. And she couldn't do either of those things. Both were much too dangerous. Not after Warren. She needed to watch the video again from the restaurant proposal—just to remind herself of her stupid, foolish heart.

No more men. Not for a long, long time.

Logan's order arrived, and he said, "Dig in, ladies," reaching for one of the sopapillas to smother it in warm honey.

"If I eat another one I'll burst," Revé said, laughing. "But I'm sure you can eat that entire order all by yourself."

He eyed it with an impish grin. "I could probably eat two orders, but it's not a very well-balanced dinner."

"Haven't you had a meal yet this evening?" Revé asked.

"Order some *dinner*," Carmen said with a roll of her eyes. The waitress passed, so Carmen quickly spoke up. "Please get this man a plate of your best burritos and rice."

"Yes, ma'am," the waitress said with a smile. "When I just saw sopapillas here, I figured you'd all had already eaten."

"This guy wants a second dinner," Carmen fibbed.

Logan's deep laugh burst out of his chest. "You are bad, Carmen Hurley," he told her.

"Just keeping you on your toes, Mr. Redmond. That's what neighbors are for."

"First time I ever heard that. I thought neighbors were for arguing over fences and leaving the trash cans out too long just to annoy each other."

"Well, that, too," Revé suddenly put in.

"You have interesting neighbors as well, Miss Chatham."

"I live in an apartment, so I have too many neighbors."

Logan's eyes were on her face. "Been a long time since I lived in an apartment with people upstairs and downstairs."

"Revé lives in the penthouse," Carmen interjected with a sly wink. "With a private elevator, twelve rooms and a maid and a butler."

"*Carmen*," Revé hissed. "Stop it!"

An interesting expression crossed Logan's face at Carmen's divulging of too much information. What did he think of Revé now? Just a spoiled heiress princess?

Carmen could have a big mouth at the most inopportune times. The problem was her friend was only half exaggerating.

The other problem was meeting an energetic and compelling man like Logan Redmond. The two of them were complete opposites, in probably every way that mattered. City girl/small town boy. Corporate job versus small business. Advanced degrees versus—well, she didn't exactly know, but Logan might not have gone to college at all.

She had wealth coming out her ears, and Logan probably barely made ends meet working at a small-town rental shop.

A melancholy feeling swept through her, but Revé quickly dismissed it. She may never find the perfect man for her, let alone the perfect kiss. That was an elusive dream that only existed in her silly, fantasy-filled mind.

She had to get used to it. This was her life. For better or worse. But Revé couldn't help wishing she'd grown up in a small town with an ordinary job as a waitress, dating the local cowboys and ranchers.

Those kinds of thoughts were stupid, too. Everyone she knew wanted to trade places with her, would kill for the wealth her family had, although her parents tried to give it away almost as fast as they made it. Their names were on the charity donations for at least a dozen orga-nizations.

"I think Revé is bored with us," Logan said, giving her a sideways grin while he dove into his steaming dinner plate of burritos smothered in a hot green chile sauce.

Revé quickly shook her head. "Of course not! Blame it on jet lag. Even though California is only one hour behind New Mexico. I'm not bored at all—but I'll apologize for being the boring one. Sorry for being such poor company."

"Not at all," Logan said gently. "Do you ladies want to see if they're dancing on the plaza?"

"The cold air would certainly wake us up after sitting in this warm restaurant for so long," Carmen said, fumbling for her purse. "But there's two of us and only one of you, Logan."

"I can dance with two women at the same time, I'm very talented that way."

"I'm sure you are," Carmen shot back. "But I'll sit it out, and you can dance with Revé and teach her our Southwestern two-step."

"Oh, no," Revé said, biting at her lip. "You don't have to hang out with us. I'm sure you have other things to do besides entertain us. Logan," she added awkwardly.

"Actually, I'm always looking for a dance partner," he said.

"Most men don't dance—or won't dance—so Logan is an anomaly, Revé," Carmen said decisively. "Grab your chance for a spin on our outdoor patio dance floor."

Revé shook her head, laughing under her breath. "You two are incorrigible."

"Thanks for letting me crash your dinner party, ladies," Logan said, throwing a couple of twenties on the table and rising to his feet.

When he stood up, his six feet four height and broad shoulders took Revé's breath away. The man was magnificent. Overcome by his presence, she was actually now dying to know what it felt like to dance with him, to be in his arms.

The three of them left the restaurant, and the cold took Revé's breath away next. Quickly wrapping a scarf around her neck, she shoved her hands into a pair of gloves and shivered on the sidewalk, admiring the Christmas lights all over again on the plaza.

"Oh, it's a different band playing now," Revé said. "I wondered how they could stand to stay outside performing for so long."

"They're playing big band Christmas music from the 40s—perfect for dancing, Miss Chatham," Logan said, offering the crook of his arm to her. "We got us a good two-step tune going right now."

"You're not going to give up, are you?" she asked, a flutter in her stomach.

"Dance with the man, Revé," Carmen urged, laughing harder. "You'll make his night, and he can die a happy man. I mean, how often does he get to dance with a sophisticated woman from California?"

"Especially a woman from the beautiful country of India?" Logan added, gazing into her face.

"I hate to burst your bubble, but I was born right here in the good old USA, actually."

The next instant, before she knew it, Logan had swept her into his arms, and they were moving about the plaza with a dozen other couples. Onlookers cheered, and Revé's face burned under the crisp evening.

Logan's skin didn't touch hers of course since they were both wearing gloves, including bulky coats that prevented any kind of contact, but when Revé tilted her head to look up into the man's face, he had eyes only for her. Eyes that grazed her lips for a brief moment, then moved away sending shivers dancing along Revé's spine.

"You *do* dance," he said in a teasing voice. "You had me fooled."

"I never said I didn't dance," she retorted with a saucy look. "My dad taught my brother and me when we were teenagers. He said it was a skill people should know— and that music and dancing was one of the pleasures of life and courtship. My parents met in a dance class, actually, in college, when my mother was here on a university scholarship."

"That's a great story," Logan said, moving her expertly about the stone pavings of Taos Plaza. Christmas lights sparkled and whirled all around them, and Revé's breath caught with the beauty of it all.

A moment later, Logan pulled her a smidgen closer,

his grip firm on her hand, the scent of his musky cologne clean and alluring. She had noted earlier that he had shaved since that morning when she first met him. Almost as if he had planned to run into them—or some other woman—tonight.

"I'm curious about something," Revé began. "I have two questions, actually."

He bent his head to look her square in the face. "I'm an open book, shoot."

"First, when were you in India? How do you know it's a beautiful country? At least parts of it. The poverty can be difficult to witness."

"Ah, you caught what I said, then. I was a missionary there once a long time ago, back in my very early twenties."

Revé staggered and missed a step, but Logan didn't let her stumble or fall. He commanded the dance floor and practically lifted her up for a brief moment to keep her on her feet. "I didn't expect you to say *that* in a million years."

Logan's smile shone under the twinkling lights, glinting off his white teeth. "I had experiences I'll never forget, and I fell in love with the people and the countryside."

"Are you trying to make me homesick for my crazy family who is probably right this very minute gossiping about my love life."

Oops, she had said too much. Revé cursed her big mouth. She had to be more careful.

"Now I *am* curious about your love life," he said, his hand tightening on hers. "I mean, if everyone is gossiping about it, it must be very juicy. Do let me in on all your secrets."

Revé swatted his arm. "Stop it. My love life is none of your business—especially my non-existent love life, Mr. Redmond. But it's nice to know that you love India, too," she added softly. "I think you're trying to make me feel guilty for not traveling there to be with my Nanni and all my aunties."

"Not at all. No guilt. I'm glad you're not there, actually. If you had gone, I never would have met you," he told her, slowly breaking their contact and giving a slight bow. "Thanks for the dance, Revé," he added gently. "I haven't danced in a long time."

That's when Revé realized the music had already stopped. For how long, she had no idea.

Carmen was at her elbow in a flash. "So, Logan," she said in a coaxing voice while batting her eyelashes. "Can we borrow your truck and your best chainsaw tomorrow? I've called everyone I know, and they're all busy. At least their trucks are busy."

"Of course. You should have asked me first. That's what neighbors are for. I'll go with you, in fact."

"We can manage the saw ourselves. Besides, we're

going to have a little picnic lunch, and I know you can't stay away from your shop for that long."

"Ah, I get it," Logan said with a crooked grin. "You two want girl's time to gossip without me around."

"Women do not gossip. I'll have you know that we discuss current events and global concerns while retrieving our Christmas pine tree."

"That's what I meant," Logan said, suppressing another smile.

"See you in the morning," Carmen called gaily while they headed back to their car parked along one of the side roads of the plaza.

Feeling eyes on her back, Revé tried not to look back over her shoulder, but her entire body felt like it had become a magnet. Charting a course to hone in on Logan Redmond.

When she and Carmen crossed the street, Revé glanced back and saw the man still standing where they had been dancing watching them get to their vehicle safely.

Briefly, she lifted a hand and Logan nodded, giving a wave in return. A fizzy, soda-pop feeling shot straight up Revé's stomach and into her throat.

The sensation of her hand in his while they'd danced amongst the shimmering lights had left a definite imprint in her palm and along the tips of her cold fingers.

CHAPTER 9

That night, Revé found herself dreaming about dancing with Logan in a close embrace amidst a flurry of snowflakes and swirling music.

She woke to bright sunshine sparkling off an inch of snow that had fallen through the night. It was gorgeous. So clean and white as if she'd dropped into the snowy world of Narnia from *The Lion, the Witch, and the Wardrobe.*

"Brr, it's *cold,*" she said to Carmen when she trotted out to the kitchen. "The window in my room is icy to the touch. I found out the hard way."

Carmen pushed a cup of hot cocoa toward her. "Let me guess. You pressed your nose to the glass to see the freshly fallen snow and got more than you bargained for."

"How did you know that?"

"Because I've done it every single time we have our first snowfall of the season since I was three years old. I never seem to learn . . ." she took a sip of her drink with a small chuckle.

"I'm feeling pleased that I packed thick socks and slippers," Revé said. "But I'm wearing them in the house!"

"I have the heat on low. I'll crank it up when we get back from cutting down our Christmas tree!"

"Can I help you pack the lunch basket?"

"Eat your eggs and shower, and then we'll pack up. I already showered but there's plenty of hot water. I turned up the thermostat on the hot water heater."

Thirty minutes later, Revé was assembling ham and cheese sandwiches, slathering them with mustard and mayo while Carmen packed chips, raw veggies, hummus, and bottles of water into a picnic hamper. She tossed in napkins, cups, and a bottle of sparkling cider, too.

"We'll stick the water and cider into a snowbank to keep cold."

"Which direction are the Christmas trees the forest service allows you to cut down?"

"We have a permit for the slopes of the Sangre de Crista east of here. About a fifteen-mile drive, but the roads are slow and bumpy in places. You'll see some spectacular views."

"Sounds fantastic. I charged my phone, so I can take lots of pictures."

"I also packed a couple of blankets into the car, too, just in case we need them."

"I guess we'll drive your car over to Logan's place to get his truck and then transfer all of our stuff over?"

"Yeah, he called this morning and said he had some customers to meet earlier than he expected."

"Oh, that's too bad," Revé began, then realized how that sounded. "I mean, it's too bad he had to go into work earlier than planned."

Carmen eyed her, a knowing look in her eyes. "You two made a pretty gorgeous couple last night dancing in the plaza. I swear there were stars in your eyes."

"Stars! Ha!" Revé spluttered. "You mean the Christmas lights reflecting off my eyes. That's all."

"Nope." Carmen shook her head. "I'm feeling . . . vibes. . . you know?"

"There's more vibes between *you* and him, than me."

"Oh, Revé, you are so cute pretending to be so innocent. Logan is like a brother to me. Honestly! I can appreciate that he's one of the best-looking men in town, but we're practically birthed from the same mother, that's how I feel about the guy. Fraternal relationship to the tenth degree! But you . . . and him . . . I see the way you're looking at him when he's not looking at you—and vice versa."

"Really?" Revé said casually, keeping her face down while she tied the laces on the snow boots Carmen had lent her, but deep down she was desperately curious.

"You don't have to pretend with me. I can see it, and I can *feel* it. Like this big cloud of enchanted attraction buzzing between you two saying, 'hey, look at me'!"

Revé waved a hand through the air. "Your imagination is too big for your head. Besides, after I leave in two weeks, then what? Absolutely nothing. We live two states apart. Our lives are worlds are apart."

"Not as different as you assume, my dear," Carmen said mysteriously.

Revé stuck a hand on her hip. "What are you talking about? I could list ten things right off the top of my head—"

Before Carmen could answer, her friend's cell phone rang, and she reached across the counter. "My mom," she whispered to Revé, covering the phone for a second before answering. "Hey, Mom, how's life on the ski slopes?"

A moment later, Carmen's face turned ashen, and she staggered into the great room, sinking onto the sofa. "What? How? Where?" The questions came all at once, and Revé's breath caught in her throat at the hoarseness in her friend's voice.

Revé sat on the ottoman across from her while Carmen didn't move an inch for the longest time.

Finally, she fell backward against the cushions, one hand against her mouth. Shock was in her eyes. "Yeah, I got it, Mom," she said, scribbling some information on the back of a magazine on the coffee table. "I'll see you in a few hours."

She hung up and lifted her head. Tears filled her hazel eyes, but she wiped them away swiftly. Carmen had never been one to cry, or get very emotional.

"Carmen, what's happened? Your mother—?"

Carmen's face had turned pale and she was breathing hard. "Mom's fine, it's my father. He had an accident skiing on a slope he shouldn't have been on. He can be such a hot dog. Well, he crashed into a tree and has a head injury and a broken leg and broken ribs. They airlifted him out, and he's going into surgery soon."

"How horrible," Revé said, shock reverberating through her. "What can I do, how can we help them?"

Carmen grabbed Revé's hand in her cold, clammy ones. "I—I'm trying to think. You barely got here yesterday."

"Don't worry about me. I'll be perfectly fine. But I could go with you and help with everything—you must be so worried and scared for your father."

Revé broke off when Carmen looked up. "Amy—my sister—is already on her way from Denver."

"I can take you to the airport," Revé said, rising to her feet. "I'll help you pack. Tell me what to do, sweetie."

Carmen's features were strained and tight. "I'd really like to be there when Dad gets out of surgery. They're in Colorado Springs. A three-hour drive. An airport won't get me there any sooner than that, so I'll take my car and then I'll have wheels to go back and forth to the hospital and a hotel."

"Are you sure you're no too upset to drive?" Revé asked, squeezing her friend's hand.

Weak laughter spilled between Carmen's lips. "Living out in the desert we drive. *A lot.* Everywhere. It's a way of life—I'm used to it—and I'm not talking about Los Angeles commutes in crappy traffic." She gave a wan smile. "Driving calms me, I can think more clearly. And I'll play soothing music. I'm more worried about deserting you after all of our great plans."

"Please don't worry about me!" Revé shook her head fiercely. "I can get myself back to Albuquerque to fly back home."

"Our Christmas together is spoiled."

Emotion filled Carmen's face. "At Dad's age . . ." her voice trailed off. "This could go so many ways. He might not survive. There are a dozen possible complications. Mom was trying not to cry on the phone in front of me, but I could hear it in her voice."

Revé tugged at her hand. "You'll feel better once you're on the road and can see him in a few hours. Just tell me how to lock up the house, and, well, everything."

Carmen paused at her bedroom door. "You know, you *could* stay right here. You don't have to go back home unless you really want to fly to India instead."

Revé gave a pained laugh. "No matter what I do, I'm not doing that. I'll, just uh, return home and pace my apartment. Maybe go to the office and do paperwork."

Carmen gave a short laugh. "You are *not* returning to California to work. Seriously, stay here. Hopefully, I can be back in a few days if everything goes well. We'll keep in touch."

She threw a suitcase on her bed and began throwing jeans, sweaters, socks, and underthings inside.

Revé helped fold and arrange while Carmen grabbed things from her closet and bureau while talking nonstop. "Okay, I'll drive my car, but my mother's Town Car is in the garage. I'll leave the keys for you. And house keys. The fridge and pantry are packed for over a week. I'll need to show you how the house alarm works. And there's a map of the town to get around somewhere in one of the junk drawers. Everybody has a junk drawer, don't they?"

Revé made a face and Carmen gave a little laugh. "Hey, even wealthy people have junk drawers, probably too many of them. My office has two filing cabinets and Alexa, my secretary ordered a third. And that's just for me alone. The main office has ten filing cabinets." She spoke lightly to distract Carmen.

"I'll worry about you, you know? But if you need help —a fire, a flood, can't get out of the driveway— there are at least three snow shovels in there—or call Logan, he'll help you. He's really just the best guy ever. I've known him my entire life."

"You've mentioned that a few times already," Revé teased.

"Um, sorry," Carmen said contritely.

The two of them turned to stare at each other, and then they burst into small laughter. But not two seconds later, Carmen burst into tears.

Revé pulled her into a hug, whispering, "He's going to be okay. He is. Take deep breaths and talk to your mom and your sister on the way so you know what's happening and that will help you feel better."

Carmen nodded shakily. "Okay. You're right. I hope you'll stay? I mean, what's waiting back home—only an ex-boyfriend who is a self-centered, horrible person. I could go on with more descriptions, but the man isn't worth it."

"Exactly. I'm avoiding home *and* India! So you might never get rid of me!"

"Oh gosh, that is too funny, Revé! I almost forgot, please go out and explore the town, too. And put up the Christmas decorations. And make sugar cookies. And watch movies. I have Netflix and Vudu and movie channels on cable. You're so smart you can probably figure out the remotes. What else?" She paused.

"And I'll remember to brush my teeth and lock the doors and not let strangers in," Revé said with a quirky smile. "And I'll only answer the phone to you. Well, I guess I'll pick up the phone to my own parents, when they call."

Carmen embraced her as they both fell into more uneasy laughter. "I'm so glad you're here, Revé. You're helping me already. I can't imagine getting this news alone. I'm okay, I really am. I'll have faith that Dad will be okay. It's just when they get to be over seventy . . ." her voice trailed away.

"Call me every day with updates, and please say hello to your mother and Amy—and your sweet dad when he wakes up."

"I will," Carmen promised, finishing packing up a toiletry bag.

Revé grabbed a jacket and a heavy coat, plus Carmen's gloves and muffler. "It was better to hear this news now during daylight hours so you can arrive before dark. Oh, I also packed some snacks for you and some of the sandwiches. Take them with you to eat on the way."

"I hadn't even thought about that, thank you, Revé."

"Maybe we'll still have Christmas together next week," she added optimistically.

After loading the Prius, they hugged one last time, and Revé waved Carmen off down the hill until she was out of sight.

Standing there for a few moments longer, she finally wrapped her arms around her cold shoulders and tramped back up the sloping lawns crusty with the fresh snow of the morning to enter the warm house.

Gazing about the beautiful sprawling home, the

silence was suddenly very thick and dense. Emotion pricked at her own eyes thinking of worst possible scenarios but knowing Carmen was more than capable of getting herself up there and being a great support to her parents.

What would *she* do if something happened to her parents? She shuddered to think about that, so Revé had to immediately banish the thoughts. Besides, it was Christmas. A time for hope and love and faith in the Savior.

Maybe she'd find a church in town to attend on Christmas Eve. Singing hymns with a congregation of worshipers would be lovely. And she could light a few luminarias on the porch, although she probably wouldn't get more than a dozen completed.

Strolling through the house, Revé took stock of the pantry, jangled the house and car keys in her fist and laid them by the front door. Double checked the alarm and instructions that Carmen had scribbled for her.

For some reason, she was famished, so she polished off the last quick-and-easy refrigerated cinnamon roll Carmen had baked that morning, feeling guilty. She needed to hike every day to burn off all these forbidden calories.

She was just playing with the television remote control when her cell phone rang. Assuming it was Carmen she snatched it up from the coffee table, shocked to see the name of Logan Redmond. How did he have her number?

"Uh-oh, guess we forgot to go pick up his truck," she said under her breath. "Um, hello?" she said into the receiver.

"Hey, Revé, good morning."

"Good morning, Logan, I'm so sorry. We should have called, but I didn't have your number—"

"No need to apologize, I just heard from Carmen. She told me about her dad. That's horrible news, and he sounds badly hurt, but I'm sure he'll be okay. Is Carmen all right? It's hard not to worry about her on the road by herself, although it *is* just a three-hour drive."

"She was a bit emotional at first, of course, but we packed in about twenty minutes, and she seemed steady to drive—after spending most of that twenty minutes assuring me that driving is not a big deal at all."

"She called just now to give me your number, I hope that's okay."

"Of course, perfectly alright," Revé said primly.

"If you need anything, please let me know. Are you —" he paused to clear his throat. "Are you going to stick around for a couple more days? I hope you're not worried about staying alone."

"I normally live alone," she said with a small laugh.

"But you're out of your familiar environment. And you still don't have a Christmas tree. It's practically a sin not to have a Christmas tree, you know."

"Is that so? Will I have to go to confession?"

Logan chuckled. "I'll take you myself."

"To confession? But's that's private, sir!"

Logan's warm, masculine laugh sent a quiver down Revé's neck. "I meant that I'll take you to chop down that pesky Christmas tree and haul it back to your house."

It was Revé's turn to chuckle over misunderstanding his meaning. "I can't ask you to do that. Besides, I don't need a Christmas tree if I'm here by myself."

"It's not Christmas until it's lit up and decorated. I'll pick you up in an hour."

"Well, I do have a cooler packed and ready. And I'm already starving for lunch even though it's only eleven."

"Be there in thirty. Maybe twenty. I'll help you eat your lunch."

"What happened to an hour?" Revé broke off when he hung up. "And now I think I need to freshen my makeup," she said aloud. "And actually fix my hair instead of this ratty ponytail."

Hurrying to her bathroom, she fixed the smudges of eyeliner and mascara after the tears with Carmen, then applied a light coat of pale pink lipstick. Finally, she pulled out the hair tie, shaking out her thick dark locks, braiding them into a double twisty swirl that hung over her shoulder.

Grabbing her coat and gloves, she hung them on the

coatrack by the front door, hauled the cooler over and peeked through the side window blinds.

Logan Redmond was pulling up at that very same moment in his rumbling diesel truck.

He'd driven up from town, not in twenty minutes, but in fifteen.

CHAPTER 10

Forty-five minutes later, Revé was trudging through knee-high powdery snow, following Logan up the side of a sloping mountain side where Douglas firs and pinon trees rose like majestic sentinels over the entire Taos valley.

The deep green color was a stark contrast to the pristine, white world of winter.

She breathed in the heady, spicy scent, her breath puffing like white smoke.

"Doing all right back there?" Logan said, turning to give her a wink with his terribly cute smile.

"Perfect," she fibbed, trying not to overheat, actually from the exertion of climbing the steep hill. Her face was cold, her nose probably red as Rudolph, but the rest of her was toasty warm from the hike. In addition to the fact that she was bundled up as fat as a snow woman. "What's the elevation here?"

"Eight thousand feet. Actually, let's take a break for a few minutes. It's thoughtless of me to make you hike in the snow at this elevation when you're used to sea level. I apologize, Revé."

She liked how he said her name, in the authentic French manner with the accent rising at the end in a long A sound. He had instinctively known how to pronounce her name, although Carmen had obviously introduced her that way initially.

"You're a trooper," Logan added. "You'll never regret your first live Christmas tree. We'll make hot chocolate when we get back, and I'll build you a fire."

"You don't need to. I saw the stacks of firewood on the side of the house, and I can build a fire with the best of them."

"How often do you build fires in southern California?"

"Oh, you'd' be surprised," she said airily. "We sometimes get down to a frigid fifty-five at night."

Logan gave a low chuckle in his throat. "I have a friend in Arizona who said the state has ruined her. After 115 degree summers, she went to turn her heater on when it came down to seventy-five degrees and found that she was pulling on a sweatshirt."

"Now that's pretty funny."

"Yeah," Logan added. "While I'm wearing shorts, she's in a jacket or a hoodie." Revé caught Logan's bottomless blue eyes, trying not to stare, but she swore they had magnets in them, forcing her gaze to return again and again to his face. Those crystal blue eyes with long eyelashes were mesmerizing. Lucky guy. His smile and easy laugh were also much too infectious and happy. "So, um, who's tending your store while you're up here searching for the perfect Christmas tree for a total stranger?"

"We're not total strangers," he contradicted. "Strangers don't dance on moonlit nights in the town square with a parade of lights just for them."

Revé quirked her lips. "Just for us, huh?"

"I like to think so." His voice quieted a little. "It was nice. You're a good dancer, Revé."

She studied his face. "Actually, so are you. Not many guys can dance well—or will even attempt it, content to make their wife or girlfriend sit on the sidelines with them at a party or dinner event."

"Too bad for them," Logan said briefly. "Dancing is very romantic."

"So you're a secret romantic?" Revé asked slyly.

"Romantic activities can also be found hiking through crazy deep snow to find the perfect tree."

"Is that what this is, Mr. Redmond?" Revé said, her gloved hands on her hips. "I thought you were doing a favor for Carmen."

"Nope, this is all for you. Carmen doesn't need my

favors or romance. We are strictly friends."

"Okay, just double-checking because if I'm not mistaken you chopped all that firewood sitting in neat stacks on the side of the house. She was surprised to see it there this morning at breakfast—before the phone call came in from her mother. Carmen suspected you'd done it."

He shrugged. "I brought it over late last night. Figured you'd need it over the next week. We have more snow predicted."

"That's very thoughtful of you, thank you."

Logan held out his hand to help Revé over a fallen tree lying in the snow. In the other hand, he held the saw. "I think I spot the perfect tree. Just a little bit more and then we'll slide down the hill."

Revé blinked. "Please tell me you're joking. Sliding or rolling down hills is for thick green lawns in the middle of the summer."

"Might be slick. Just a warning," he teased. "You can hang on to me."

"I'm sure I'll manage perfectly fine on my own," she said casually, but as they walked another hundred yards, he crooked a smile at her confidence but didn't reply. As if he knew a secret she didn't.

"What do you think of this beauty?" Logan asked, shading his eyes to gaze up at the tall Douglas fir with thick foliage and vibrant green colors.

"Wow, I think it's the best one yet," Revé agreed,

circling the base. "Perfectly symmetrical on all sides. Good for decorating."

"Okay, the lady has made her choice," Logan announced to the world. "Stand back while I cut it down. Don't want flying shrapnel to get you."

Stepping back, Revé gave him space while she surveyed the Taos village below, lying quiet as if its inhabitants had all gone in for an afternoon siesta.

Those rippling muscles hiding underneath Logan's heavy coat could only be imagined, but it didn't take more than ten minutes for the tree to go falling into the deep snow, a soft shushing sound as a flurry of snow rose in the air, catching the sunlight.

Revé clapped her hands with the success and then sloshed through the deep snow to help Logan tie a length of rope he'd brought to secure the tree and drag it back down the hill.

"My toes have gone numb," she mused aloud. "I can't feel them." The next second, she let out a startled cry when her boots slipped underneath her as she stepped on an icy spot and went straight down on her back—then immediately began sliding all the way down the hill.

Arms flailing, Revé tried to stop herself, but the entire world was slippery like wet glass, and there was nothing to grab but powdery snow all around her. Picking up speed, she finally managed to twist her body over onto her stomach to attempt to claw her way to a halt.

Which was useless. She continued to slide and Revé tried not to panic, despite the sudden cry bursting out of her throat.

In an instant, Logan was beside her, sliding feet first while still holding the rope, then throwing his legs over hers to stop her speed.

Revé found herself on her back, staring up at the bright sky. She closed her eyes for a moment, relieved that she wasn't in danger of going over a cliff—or hitting the muddy road or Logan's truck.

His soft laughter sounded in her ear as he rolled closer to her side. "Well, that's one way to get the tree down the mountain faster."

"It was all a part of my diabolical plan," she said, panting, her breath coming in gasps.

"Honestly, are you okay?" Logan asked.

"Hit an ice spot," she said, her panicked breaths finally slowing.

"No sprains or twisted knees?"

"I don't think so, but I'm not sure if I trust myself to get up again. How close is the truck?"

"About thirty yards."

"Piece of cake," Revé said, trying to keep her sense of humor.

"Yum. Have you got cake back at the house?" Logan's

voice was hopeful, like a kid, which made Revé roll her eyes and burst out with a laugh.

"Can you only think of your stomach at a time like this, Mr. Redmond?"

"Always. My stomach wants to be fed every two hours. That's what my mother used to say."

"Actually, I'm pretty hungry, too. The food basket is still safe, right?"

"Let's eat in the car. I'll turn the heater on full blast."

"You got yourself a deal, buddy. But I'm not sure if I can walk with frozen toes. It feels like my entire body stopped functioning properly." Revé's teeth began to chatter from the frigid air.

Not three seconds later, Logan was on his feet. Before she knew it, he was swinging Revé up into his arms and carrying her down the mountain.

Revé's face burned with embarrassment. "Oh, good grief put me down, I'm not an invalid!"

"No, but you're light as a feather, and you said that nothing was working, so I did what came naturally."

"You are a big jokester, aren't you, Mr. Redmond?"

"I like to have fun and not take life too seriously. But I can be very sober when the occasion needs it," he added, putting on a grave face as if he were at a funeral.

That just made Revé laugh all over again. "You've already spent way too much time helping me out. Just to get a Christmas tree. Something temporary and frivolous."

"I must disagree, Miss Chatham. Christmas trees are mighty solemn matters of business. Here we are," Logan said, opening the passenger door to place her carefully on the seat and helping her swing her frozen legs inside.

His warm hands on her calves and feet practically made Revé jump into the roof of the truck with a powerful electric charge that completely discombobulated her. She stared at his beautiful hair and perfect mouth. His face was mere inches from hers as he spread a blanket over her legs.

His nearness made Revé's stomach jump straight up her throat. When Logan glanced into her face, she felt him give a start as if he didn't realize their heads were so close either.

His breath was warm on her skin, his fresh scent intoxicating. Dizzy, she closed her eyes, inwardly chiding herself to ignore all incoming sensory overload.

When Revé flashed her eyes open again, she found Logan gazing at her, a slow smile on his lips, his arms tucking a blanket around her. She was safe and warm on this dangerous snowy mountain. It was the strangest feeling to be so calm and peaceful, enjoyable in a way she had never experienced with another man.

They didn't speak, just stared at each other while time seemed to stand still, even though only a few seconds had passed.

A moment later, Revé squealed and sat up. "Oh, oh,

oh! There's—what is that? Snow is crawling down my neck—and now my back. It's *freezing!!* Ah!"

Revé jumped out of the truck, flinging off the blanket and trying to shake her clothes out, but the snow was melting fast, creating an awful icy dribble while goosebumps broke out over her entire body.

"Snow is *crazy!*" she squealed, and then realized that Logan was laughing at her. He watched her dance around in circles while unsuccessfully attempting to extract the melting snow without shedding all of her clothes in the frigid temperature.

Revé glared at him. "Did you put snow down my neck? You did, didn't you? You sneak!"

"No, I promise, I didn't," Logan said, holding up his hands in innocence before bending down to roll a handful of snow into a ball. "But right now is a great time for a snowball fight, don't you think?"

"What?!" Revé stood stock still, knee-high in the icy cold stuff just as Logan threw his snowball and got her right in the arm. The snowball splattered, throwing powder into the air and sparkling under the sun. "You asked for it now!" she shouted at him, a tremulous smile spreading across her face.

This was so crazy. They were like kids again, and Revé was doing something she'd never dreamed she ever would, but Logan was so easy to be with, actually. She became aware of how relaxed she was, and how much fun she was having. The desire to spend the entire day with him was growing stronger every minute.

Quickly, she bent down and picked up two handfuls of snow, smashing them together to smack Logan right in the chest. "Bulls-eye!" she crowed, clapping her hands, although the man never even flinched.

"Good shot," Logan said, admiration in his voice, but his words were merely a distraction to her ego, because his next snowball came almost immediately, smacking Revé in the thigh.

Soon the snowballs were flying back and forth, and Revé found herself running back and forth to form snowballs while trying to avoid getting hit, and then falling over in her boots as she tried not to trip when each footstep sank into deep snow holes of the powdery stuff.

After twenty hits, she lost count of her throws and, suddenly exhausted, she fell over and lay there, laughing harder than she had in ages.

A second later, Logan fell beside her on his back, and they were both gasping from the exertion, trying to catch their breaths.

Logan turned his head to look at Revé. "You make a good opponent. You sure you've never had a snowball fight before?"

"Never in my life, but I have an older brother, and we used to play softball growing up. Catch in the backyard under the maple trees."

"I never would have thought a big shot executive like you would have played in the backyard like that. Figured you'd be at violin lessons. Attending teas and structured play dates. Spending time on college resumes and in the limelight crowned as Homecoming Queen by the time you were a senior."

Revé gave him a smirk, rolling on her side so they were facing each other. "So you think I'm just a big snob? Wow. I don't know whether you're mocking me or complimenting me."

His lips twitched as if trying not to laugh. "Maybe a little of both."

"What did you do while growing up? Play with toy trucks, go hot-rodding with your friends while wearing sweaty cowboy hats?"

"Touché, Revé," he said with an amused chuckle. "You just are not what I was expecting when Carmen told me about her friend coming out for Christmas. She was bragging on you and your brilliant family and wealth."

Revé sat up, brushing snow from her gloves and wrapping her arms around her knees as she looked out over the valley of never-ending mountains in every direction.

"Well, just for your information, my family wasn't this—successful? Or whatever you want to call it." She bit at her lips and noticed his eyes dropping to her mouth, before quickly rising back to her eyes. A ticklish sensation ran up and down her spine in a provocative manner.

"Tell me more," he said. "You've got me curious."

Logan's eyes were burning heat and fire through Revé, and she was having a difficult time processing her thoughts, trying not to stumble over her words like a teenager.

"I don't know what you'd call my family now. We weren't 'rich'—certainly not for many years. My parents struggled to pay bills and pay for my piano lessons. And then my father finished his Ph.D. and fell into some connections in the pharmaceutical field. He had some great ideas, and his research team followed, and then he became head of the lab—and then owned the lab when he made some brilliant decisions. I don't call that luck and being born into money. Just hard work."

"Sounds like God was pouring blessings down on your family."

A tentative smile crossed Revé's lips as she nodded. "I agree about God's hand directing your life. Putting you in the right place at the right time. Like now."

Logan's eyebrows lifted, and he seemed to inch closer to her. "What do you mean?"

"Meaning I had to get away from California or throw myself off a bridge. At the moment though, if I don't get down this hill, I'm going to stay stuck and frozen to this mountain for the rest of my life."

A small flash of disappointment crossed his eyes, and

Revé wondered what it meant. Was he truly experiencing the same attraction to her that she was to him?

The idea was gratifying, but Revé shook her head as she rose to her frigid feet and brushed off her wet jeans that had frozen to her legs, despite the waterproof snow pants Carmen had let her borrow.

She told herself to get over it and move on with her life—and her heart. Logan Redmond was not the man for her. It was impossible. They had completely different experiences. They couldn't be more different. Polar opposites, 180 degrees apart.

Yes, he was one of the best-looking men she had ever seen in her life. Yes, he sent tingles of desire and romance all over her body, but any sort of future relationship wasn't going to happen. So she had to just forget the ideas jumping into her mind and heart.

"We haven't made snow angels yet," Logan told her, still sitting in the snowbank. "Bet you've never done one before."

She shot him a look. "You're right, I haven't. Isn't that for kids?"

"Any kid up to ninety years old."

"Are you daring a girl from Southern California?"

"You bet I am."

Revé plopped down again in the hollow she had made earlier and spread her arms and legs, moving them in and out across the snow. "Is this how it's done? I have seen movies, you know."

All at once Revé began to slide as the snow turned to slick ice. "Whoa!" she said, trying to stop herself. But all at once, she was slipping faster down the side of the hill for the second time that day clutching at the icy mounds of snow. "Help!" she yelped.

Instantly, Logan was on his knees and grabbing at her hands to pull her back. She scrambled awkwardly, feeling like a big, ungainly hippo and completely ungraceful.

Within moments, Logan had her back in the deeper snow where ice hadn't formed yet, and she could stand again on solid ground.

"I'm no ice skating star, that's for sure," Revé said self-deprecatingly.

"It happens to everyone at one time or another. It's just your lucky day."

It was then that Revé realized he was still holding her firmly, so she didn't keep slipping. Despite their bulky clothing, the man was warm and big-chested and strong. They had both gone quiet, gazing at each other.

Revé stuttered at the magnetic pull of his eyes and his irresistible nearness. "So um—how did my snow angel turn out?"

Logan gestured to the ground. "Looks like a lopsided swan trying to fly across a pond. And mine looks like a demon."

"That must mean you have a devilish streak," she couldn't resist saying.

"Good one, Revé," he said, his voice warm and rich.

The timbre of it struck something strange and beautiful in her chest.

"Okay," Logan said next. "Hang on to me, we're going to get down the hill without falling—and retrieve our Christmas tree. Although the tree slid closer to the truck while we had our snowball fight. Won't take long to get it up in the truck."

A few minutes later, Revé was inside the truck, the heater going full blast while Logan tied the pine tree into the truck bed, securing it up along the roof where it hung over the windshield a foot.

"We're not going far," Logan said, giving her a smile. "I'll have you home soon. Thawing out yet?"

"Oh, yes. But I'm starving."

"We deserve our lunch before heading home," he agreed.

Pulling out the picnic hamper, they ate ravenously while talking about their jobs and childhood and college experiences.

"And now," Logan said, crumpling up a napkin and offering her the last of the hot cocoa. "I'm dying of curiosity. What did you mean when you said you had to get away from California or throw yourself off a bridge? That sounds ominous."

Revé stared out the windshield. "Did Carmen spill all my secrets?"

"Not at all. She doesn't gossip. But when you said

that, something tugged at me. Your voice—there was hurt there. I want to know more—I want to know more about *you*, a woman I find intriguing. Not to mention stunningly gorgeous."

Revé hoped her face wasn't bright red as she blushed furiously at his compliments. While hearing his words were lovely and exactly what she desperately needed to hear after Warren's infidelity, she couldn't entertain any feelings for this man. He was an elusive, impossible fantasy.

"Logan, thanks for the compliments, but as nice as you are, we're just too different. Today was a one-off sort of day. We were just getting a tree and goofing around. And—I—I can't talk about my life. It's too complicated and hopeless. Can you just take me back to the house, please?"

CHAPTER 11

ell, she'd utterly ruined their day in the snow, Revé thought with a huge deflating sigh when she hauled the picnic basket into Carmen's kitchen to unload the leftovers and put things away.

Plopping the remains of lunch all over the counter, she figured she had completely blown any sort of friendship with Logan for the next two weeks. She shouldn't have said what she did in the truck, making it sound like he meant nothing to her when he had been good and kind to her.

The house was already feeling lonely and too quiet. She missed Carmen. And she missed her family, picturing them landing in New Delhi and packing themselves into her grandmother's tiny car to zoom along the crowded streets up to her house on the hill.

Everybody talking a mile a minute and laughing and catching up.

Had she been foolish not going with her parents to India? That's probably where she belonged, not here, despite Taos' beauty and the winter wonderland of the mountains.

She desperately wanted a long, hot soak in the tub to thaw her limbs and toes, but first she called Carmen, punching the buttons on her phone.

"Hey, Carmen, did you make it to Colorado okay? How's your father?"

"He just got out of surgery, and the doctors said it went well. Mom and I haven't seen him yet because he's in recovery and not awake. I'll call you after I know more, okay?"

Carmen sounded distracted, and Revé could hear voices in the background at the hospital.

"I understand, I don't want to take you away from your mom. She needs you."

"I promise to call you later. Thanks for checking in. I miss you already."

"Me, too," Revé whispered. "Hang in there and give my love to your parents—and some huge thanks for letting me stay here."

She clicked off just as the back door to the outside patio opened. It was Logan hauling the Christmas tree inside. Revé had tried so hard to put him out of her mind, she was startled at the sight of him. Of course, he'd bring in the tree for her!

"Hey, Revé, where do you want it?" he called out.

She hurried out from the kitchen and surveyed the great room with its vast ceilings. "My enormous pine tree suddenly shrunk in half!"

"That always happens when you get a live tree home. It either doubles in size if you have a small place like I do—or shrinks when there are twenty-foot-tall ceilings like the Hurley house."

"How about next to the fireplace—if we just move this armchair closer to the sofa arrangement?"

Logan nodded and set the tree in place. He'd already created a base for the trunk so it wouldn't topple over. When he'd made it, Revé wasn't sure, but the man was fast. He'd probably done it in the garage while she'd been in the kitchen on the phone and putting their picnic leftovers away.

He slowly spun the tree in place. "Which side looks best?"

"Right there," she said, pointing. "This side facing us is fuller, and the emptier space can go against the wall."

Logan set the tree, checked the stand, and stepped back. "I agree. It's perfect. And still over ten feet tall, which is a big tree for most houses."

"It must have been awfully heavy to load and carry in here."

He shook his head, his eyes smiling at her. "Piece of cake."

Staring at his large stature and muscles, Revé could see why. He moved things about easily, not even breathing hard—except for when they'd been rolling down the snowy hills and tumbling into each other in the frosty air.

Revé thought about that. She had to stop reliving their day together. She had to cut off any magnetic attraction she'd been having because she knew it would go absolutely nowhere.

"How can I ever thank you for all your help?" she said now, forcing her voice to sound nonchalant. "I feel guilty keeping you away from your shop. It's probably a busy time of year, huh?"

"Yes, but I have good employees, and I was glad to help you out. Thanks for lunch, too." He stepped closer for a moment as if wanting to say more, but then stopped himself. "Stop in and say hello anytime, Revé."

There was his marvelous voice sounding out her name again. She melted a little but steadied herself against the back of one of the leather couches. "Sure. Yeah, of course."

As if changing his mind about his distance from her, Logan suddenly crossed the living room, definitively moving closer now. His blue eyes riveted to her brown ones. "I hope I didn't offend you with my questions earlier," he said, his voice softer. "Just wanted to get to know you better. I'm here if you need me, for anything. I got ladders for changing lightbulbs, a tool kit for fixing the fridge, a mechanic's hat for your car engine."

"You're a very talented man," she said, unable to stop herself from smiling back at him in return. His smile was infectious and grew even wider at hers. There was a moment of startling quiet as they drank each other in.

Revé finally broke off the gaze. "Um, well, have a good day. Thanks again."

Logan nodded, heading to the door. "Hang on a second, I'll be right back."

Revé frowned, wondering what he was up to. Two minutes later, he appeared again with an armload of chopped firewood, plopping the logs into a box next to the fireplace.

When he straightened, he said, "Can't spend a Christmas in Taos without a good fire."

"That's perfect, thank you. Logan," she added, testing his name on her tongue.

"I can build and set the fire for you, too," he suggested.

Revé shook her head. "I'm good. This city girl can actually build a fire. My dad taught me. When we used to go camping. Before life—and the pharmaceutical world—got insanely crazy."

He nodded sagely. "I know a bit about crazy. But don't forget to take time to enjoy a fire—or go rolling down a snowy hill to make a snow angel."

"I even know what kindling is," she informed him, her lips tipping into a smile she couldn't stop.

"I never doubted it," he replied, as if amused and delighted by her all at the same time. He tipped his cowboy hat and headed toward the front door. "Have a good afternoon, Revé. Build your rip-roaring fire and relax with a good book. It sounds like you deserve a vacation. And tell Carmen and her parents hello from the crew and me. Please give them my best."

"I will," she promised, following him to the door.

After saying goodbye, she held the door open just a sliver to watch him walk down the driveway back to his truck.

As if sensing that she was still there, Logan turned to give a quick wave before sliding into the driver's seat and bringing the engine to life in an obnoxious rumbling growl.

Revé slammed the door shut and leaned against it, emotion pricking at her eyelids. What a bewildering morning. What a bewildering man. Why was her heart pounding like a jackhammer and her cheeks flushed and hot?

Why did she want to call him back to build her that fire and curl up on the sofa to talk the afternoon away? She had no doubt that they could talk for hours. She was extremely curious about the man, and he appeared to be so with her, too.

But she couldn't reveal her true self. Her real reason

for being here. That she was on the rebound, her heart scarred. Her personal life that was constantly a mess.

Despite having on-target intellectual instincts with the medical world, her own brain couldn't seem to make good choices when it came to men and love.

It was clear that she and Logan had way too many obstacles between them. Insurmountable obstacles. The sooner she accepted that fact, the better off she'd be. No more daydreaming about Logan Redmond. She had failed at every relationship, and this would be no different, just more heartache so why even try? Besides, she'd be going back to California in less than two weeks, never to see him again.

"Get over it," Revé whispered, dropping onto the couch and laying a hand over her eyes with emotion she couldn't control any longer. "Logan Redmond ceases to exist."

CHAPTER 12

The next morning, snowflakes were lightly falling out of a gray sky—and yet just beyond the mountains the clouds were breaking up, and a bright blue sky shone through the cracks. How funny to have two different kinds of weather at the very same moment.

Carmen had often said that in New Mexico, if the weather was terrible, just wait five minutes and it would change.

Seeing that bright blue sky so close was hopeful, and Revé tried not to let her melancholy mood color all her emotions. It was Christmas, she should be celebrating. Enjoying a break from her hectic, stressful life. Hours of quiet and reading and baking cookies were proving restorative.

Except that if she ate too many cookies—when the

recipe made three dozen—the flight attendants would have to roll her onto the airplane after New Year's.

Revé was determined to find neighbors or Carmen's friends to give her cookies and gingerbread to. She'd run into town and grab some holiday plates, plastic wrap, and bows at the local Walgreens. She'd take a walk later this afternoon when it was a few degrees warmer and deliver them to the neighbors and introduce herself.

Carmen had called again the previous evening when Revé had finally gotten a fire going and was watching *It's a Wonderful Life* while eating soup. She really should have let Logan build it for her. It appeared that her fire-making skills had gone quite rusty. It had taken a good hour to finally get it going to warm up the house.

"Dad's slowly waking up from the anesthesia," Carmen had told her. "And Mom has finally stopped breaking down into tears. The doctors said the surgery went well, but recovery is going to be slow. There's nothing they can do for broken ribs, it's just a painful, long road for them to heal. His broken leg will take three months, and it turns out he got a hairline fracture in his hip. No hip replacement needed, but bed rest and physical therapy. And yet, he can't do much physical therapy until the femur heals more in a few weeks."

"Wow, how frustrating," Revé said. "Sounds like it's going to take many months for him to get well. What can I do to help? I feel so badly that I'm not there with you to run errands or pick up food so you can stay at the hospital."

"Mom is so distracted she needs me to remind her to eat and sleep. Honestly, there's nothing up here. You'd just be staring at the four walls. I'm actually thrilled that you're at the house. I don't have to worry about it being unoccupied or the pipes freezing. In my rush to leave, I probably would have forgotten to lock the doors or set the alarm."

"Glad I could help, at least it's something," Revé replied, feeling better about being useful.

"In fact," Carmen said slowly. "Is there any chance you can stay past New Year's—at least for a few days? I'm going to stay up here and help Mom keep Dad's spirits up, make sure he's getting the best care—and keep Mom from breaking down. And pester the doctors with questions," she added with a laugh. "Dad's having some allergic reactions to some of the meds, too, but we'll figure it out, although it's making my mother pretty worried. He actually had an asthma attack last night, and his blood pressure dropped pretty low. I won't bore you with all the details, but I really can't leave. I'll just do a tiny Christmas up here for them both and decorate the hospital room to lift their spirits."

"Oh, my gosh, Carmen, that sounds even worse than I imagined. Especially when you first thought that it was just a broken leg. *Of course,* I'll stay and house-sit. That's the easy part. Don't worry about a thing down here. I'm blasting Christmas music, sharpening my fire-making skills and eating too many cookies. I'll make a few more batches and freeze some for you all when you get home. And I'll assemble a few casseroles and freeze them, too."

Carmen really laughed at that. "*My* Revé baking in the kitchen? All I remember is that in our college apartment your cooking skills were so bad you burned microwave popcorn."

"Hey, in my defense, it's easy to burn popcorn in the microwave. Just adding an extra ten seconds does it."

"You just proved my point, girl." Carmen's laughter subsided. "Seriously, you are a lifesaver for hanging out in Taos for so long. I hope it doesn't interfere too much with your own work schedule."

"My family is gone until New Year's Eve, and the office is on a half-time schedule. Alexa, my assistant, knows to call me with anything she can't handle. It'll be fine."

"That makes me feel less guilty. Hey," Carmen added. "Don't let Logan drive you too crazy, either. I can see him making up excuses to stop by for one thing or the other."

"Why would he do that?" Revé asked innocently.

"I haven't seen him stare at a woman as much as he did you in a long time. Years probably. I think he might be smitten, my dear," Carmen said gaily.

"You're crazy. Smitten? That's such an old-fashioned word," Revé said, brushing it off.

"I know the truth when I see it. Maybe you're just an exotic female specimen to the guy. You are pretty gorgeous, you know."

"Stop it! You're making up stories. Logan and I— we're completely different, and I live eight hundred miles away. Besides, don't you know that Revé Chatham doesn't know how to pick a man, not even if the right one was staring her in the face?"

"I'm not convinced yet," Carmen said vaguely. "Maybe I think you two have more in common than you think you do."

"Prove it."

"I'll have to prove it another time, the doctor just walked in with a specialist. Bye!"

And just like that Carmen was gone.

Revé tossed her cell phone onto the couch and sighed, staring through the French doors that opened onto the back patio and the mountains. Snowflakes drifted through the air like magical butterflies.

She didn't think she could ever get tired of such a stunning view. It made her realize how stifling and downright ugly so much of Los Angeles was. At least the inner city was with its congested freeways and aging buildings.

Taos was literally a breath of fresh air. She could see forever and the scenery was like a vivid painting the colors were so breathtaking with perfect views as if God had made it his personal divine handiwork.

"I probably could live here," she whispered aloud, ruminating on how much better she was sleeping the past two nights alone. There was a rejuvenating and restorative ambiance, even when she was icy cold and had snowballs melting down her neck.

Two hours later, Revé was about to begin another Christmas Hallmark movie when she found herself staring up at the tall evergreen she and Logan had chopped down the day before.

"If I'm going to be here for the next two weeks I'm going to decorate that poor, bare tree. I spent a lot of energy getting it home—despite suffering a snowball fight with Logan Redmond," she mused, the remote control frozen in her hand. It almost hurt to say his name, but Revé brushed the man out of her thoughts.

She didn't intend to start rummaging through the Hurley's two sheds in the rear grounds of the property in an attempt to find Christmas decorations. She'd probably turn into a popsicle after fifteen minutes.

She could hit the big box stores up the road, but then what would she do with hundreds of dollars of Christmas decorations after the New Year? She couldn't pack them into her suitcase.

And then she had a brilliant idea.

Grabbing her phone, Revé began searching for the name of the rental store. She could *rent* a Christmas! The decorations, the lights, the tinsel. Couldn't she?

Revé sooooo wanted a real Christmas and Carmen

had mentioned a few days ago that Logan's place was a full-service rental store. Or did that just refer to renting out refrigerators and recliners and Xboxes on 12-month plans? Well, she'd just go find out.

Plus, she was ready for a jaunt out of the house. She had to do something with her free time, and books and movies and cookies only went so far after a few days.

Besides, Revé had always loved how beautifully her mother decorated their house for the holidays. The smell of cinnamon and pine and gingerbread. She wanted that—she needed that.

After a quick bite of lunch, Revé finished dressing in something other than sweatpants and fixed her hair and face.

Grabbing her handbag and the car keys, she headed out into the winter wonderland that surrounded the house.

The shock of the cold air hit her in the face, and she shivered uncontrollably until the Town Car warmed up. At least she didn't have to scrape ice off the windows since it was in the garage.

Fifteen minutes later she was out of the foothills and passing the plaza area of town. Down Highway 68 was the Walmart and just beyond that lay Redmond Rentals.

"Wow," Revé said. "This is bigger and nicer than I expected."

The store logo was in big red letters, and it was well-kept, the parking lot more than half-filled.

Sucking in a breath and wondering if she'd run into a certain Mr. Redmond himself, Revé pushed through the double glass doors, her stomach in her throat.

A cozy warmth hit her face, and she gazed about at the appliances and furniture and electronics that were available for rent. When she'd parked two minutes earlier, she'd also spotted outdoor furniture and a yard full of heavy equipment to rent.

Looked like Logan covered all the bases for his customer. This wasn't a small homespun shop at all with shelves full of old clocks and toys and paraphernalia.

"May I help you?" came a voice. An older man with silver hair that reminded Revé of her father stood there wearing slacks, a pressed buttoned shirt, and tie.

"I—I'm new in town and just checking you out. May I wander around a bit?"

"Of course, as long as you'd like. If there's something specific, just let me know. We have an even larger room in the back with outdoor items and anything you'd need for your house. Right now, we have lots of Christmas specials, too. I'll check back with you in a bit."

He turned to go but not before Revé spotted the gentleman's nametag—Keith Redmond. Was he Logan's brother, an uncle, a cousin, or his father?

When she turned to wander down the aisles, she muttered to herself, "Doesn't matter who he is. Logan doesn't exist, remember?"

Redmond's Rental had nice things, plus high-tech

items, but also smaller items to rent like games and blenders, microwaves, and Christmas china. There was even an entire display of fake Christmas trees in every size, but none of the trimmings. Folks probably went to Wal-Mart for all the ribbons and big red bows.

Revé found herself craning her neck around each new aisle she wandered to see if she could spot Logan. When she realized what she was doing she immediately chided herself for being such an idiot over a man. But she missed his smile, his warm laughter, and his teasing comments. Logan was smart and quick, too.

Carmen had mentioned in passing that he was an alumnus of Arizona State University with a Master's Degree in Computer Engineering. So why was the man not working at a big tech company or Los Alamos Laboratories?

Shaking her head, Revé turned the last corner and ran smack into Keith Redmond again. "Oh, pardon me."

"Find anything you like?" he asked, his voice deep like her own father's. She found that she missed her dad. They worked so closely together it was hard not to see him every day.

"Lots of things I like, but I actually don't need anything here. I was hoping—um, it just sounds silly."

"Nothing is silly. We can make any dream come true."

Revé laughed. Was that just a salesman's pitch? But he sounded sincere.

"I mean it," he went on. "We can do pretty much anything. You mentioned that you're new in town? Are you outfitting a new house or redecorating?"

"No, nothing like that. I'm house-sitting for the Hurley's while they're in Colorado."

"Oh yes, Doctor Hurley and his family are good friends of ours. My son is their neighbor."

"So, you're, um, Logan's father?"

He nodded, smiling at her. 'Guess you've met him then?"

"He helped me chop down a Christmas tree yesterday."

"That sounds like Logan. He has a hard time being cooped up inside. I heard about Stan Hurley's skiing accident. When do they get home?"

"Not for a few weeks, so I'm staying on. I'm Carmen's friend from ages ago in college. It's my first time in New Mexico, and it's gorgeous."

Mr. Redmond grew thoughtful. "What would you like to rent? We'll call it a friends and family special."

"Oh, please, you don't have to do that. This might sound silly, but what I really want to do is—is *rent* a *Christmas*. The whole thing. The decorations, the ornaments, the candles—the miniature Victorian Christmas village that lights up. Oh, and luminarias for Christmas Eve!"

Mr. Redmond's smile grew at her enthusiasm, but he looked regretful. "We don't usually carry any of that, but

I'll pass it along to my staff. I'm so sorry. Try Wal-Mart or Walgreens, places like that. They carry it all."

"It was just a whim," Revé said, trying to shake off the dream. "It just wouldn't feel like Christmas without a houseful of kids either, right? Grown-up Christmases aren't near as much fun."

"I can attest to that," he said, nodding with a chuckle that sounded exactly like Logan's laugh. A searing sensation blasted Revé right in the heart. "My wife and I are blessed to have several grandchildren who come and spend the night in their new pajamas on Christmas Eve."

Homesickness pricked at Revé's eyes. She blinked them back. "Thank you for your time—and indulging my fantasy."

"Come back and see us any time," Mr. Redmond called out, walking her to the door.

Revé climbed into the car laughing ruefully at herself. "Silly girl. Now go grocery shopping and make some more cookies and you'll be just fine."

CHAPTER 13

After gorging on fresh-baked lemon bars, Revé was startled when the doorbell rang.

She peeked through the side curtains of the front door glass windows and turned on the porch light.

Logan stood there rubbing his hands in his thick gloves, his breath coming out in puffs of white clouds. She didn't realize that it was already dusk.

When she opened the door, his eyes were on her face and he was so darn handsome she couldn't quite catch her breath.

"Revé," he said, a slow smile spreading across his face.

Her stomach jumped into her throat, and her heart began to beat wildly. "Logan, what are you doing here?"

"I've brought you Christmas."

She cocked her head, wondering if she'd heard him correctly. "What are you talking about?"

"My dad told me you came into the shop and wanted to rent Christmas, so I'm delivering it."

"What?! You're—that's crazy!"

Revé watched with utter bewilderment as two young men began unloading a small trailer attached to the back of Logan's big black monster truck. Brown cardboard boxes of tree ornaments in every sparkly, glitter-dusted color arrived, including tinsel and red and gold garland were soon stacked beside her Christmas tree.

There was a Christmas village that Logan placed on the table and plugged in. Golden light lit up the windows of the steepled church, including Santa's workshop and various houses including a bed and breakfast hotel.

Tiny lampposts lined the street and a sparkly white "snow" cloth for the ground underneath the village. Miniature townsfolk and figurines of singing carolers were going door to door carrying wreaths. Two small old-fashioned cars completed the picture of a time long gone in the past.

"It's absolutely magnificent," Revé breathed. "So exquisite and charming. It makes me want to shrink super tiny and dive right in to go singing Christmas carols with the neighbors."

"You don't have to turn yourself into a miniature person to go caroling or take cookies to your hungry neighbors," Logan told her with a wink of those amazing blue eyes of his.

He was right—and hinting broadly.

"I'll make up a plate of the cookies I baked this morning for you to take home," she told him, trying not to laugh at the man.

"Now you're talking! I smelled the gingerbread as soon as the door opened. Here's a star for the top of your tree," Logan said next, hooking it up to an extension cord and reaching up to place it on the tallest branch—without a step ladder. "Flip the switch," he added.

Revé plugged it in and pressed the button. The star shot out rays of brilliant light all around the room, sparking off the table lamps and the chandelier over the dining room table off to the side. "Oh, that's gorgeous!"

There was another box that held Santa and Mrs. Claus, including a sleigh and a team of reindeers to decorate the entryway table. A smaller, already lit and decorated tree went on the table behind the sofa grouping, and green and red garland and lights for the mantle.

It didn't take long to place everything with Revé directing the location of each item and plugging in the electric cords while Logan set it all up. Except for the tree. She'd take her time to decorate that over the next day or two.

Logan thanked his delivery guys, and after a chorus of thank you's and Merry Christmas, they jumped back into the rental company truck and drove down the hill again.

Revé closed the front door, suddenly sucking in air at the sight of Logan still standing in front of her, tall and gorgeous, a faint musky cologne spicing the air. Or maybe that was the apple cider simmering on the stove.

"Last, but not least," Logan said softly, holding out a covered cardboard box for Revé to take.

"What is this?" she said, giving him a sideways look.

"Just open it. Aren't you a woman who loves surprises?"

Revé set the box on the coffee table and opened the flaps. Inside were a hundred small paper bags and four boxes of short, fat white candles totaling one hundred as well. She glanced up at Logan and gave him a half-smile. "Gosh, thanks, but I'm still confused. What *is* this?"

"Your very own luminaria-making kit," he told her. "Except there aren't actual kits to purchase. Luminarias are much more homemade than that. Just paper lunch bags with the tops folded down an inch or two, then scoop a cup of sand into the bottom of the bag to keep it anchored to the ground. The candle sits in the center of the sand. Here's a long-handled lighter to light the candles on Christmas Eve."

"That's so simple but so amazing. Where do I get the sand?"

"Well, we usually just head out to the desert and bring it back in a wheelbarrow, but I brought you a twenty-pound sack. It takes a couple of hours, but I'll help you. We'll place them along the driveway, the walkways, and the edges of the flower beds. Some people even put them along the edge of their roofline for a 3-D effect."

"It sounds absolutely beautiful."

Logan smiled at her and nodded. "I promise it will be one of the prettiest sights you'll ever see for Christmas anywhere. After we get all yours lit up, I'll take you down to the town plaza to see it ablaze with ten thousand luminarias."

"That sounds . . . beyond remarkable," Revé said, trying to imagine the spectacular sight. "But Logan, I'm flabbergasted that you brought all this over. And," she stuck a hand on her hip. "I *know* your rental store didn't have any of this to rent. Please don't tell me you went out and bought all this."

He moved closer, a playful look on his face. "Actually, I had most of it in one of our overflow sheds on the back of the property."

"You liar," she shot back, trying not to smile, but his grin was infectious, and lit up his face. Revé fought the tug in her body that made her hunger to move closer to him.

Instead, she braced a hand on one of the side tables to remain where she was and not launch into his arms. "You are a very sweet and generous man," she said softly.

Logan continued to surprise her and delight her, and

she was getting to the point where she wanted to spend all of her time with him.

"Just enjoy it, Revé. Since you're stuck here alone for a couple of weeks, you needed to have Christmas, too."

She lifted her shoulders in a shrug. "Oh, I would have survived. After all, I've already eaten five pounds of cookies today. I might try making fudge tomorrow."

"Save some for me? With the holiday rush in full swing, I don't get to take a lunch break much."

"Fudge for lunch?" she asked, quirking her lips at him. "Of course, but I can't guarantee my first attempt will be edible." There was a pause, and Revé said, "I met your dad at the store. He was really nice. Reminds me of my dad. He put you up to this, didn't he?"

Logan lifted his eyebrows with a low chuckle. "I admit that he told me about you coming in. I was out on delivery at the time and sorry to miss you."

"You don't rent this stuff, do you? It's all things you can purchase at any big box superstore."

"That's what made it easy to get."

"I knew it!" Revé pointed a finger at him, giving him a stern look. "How much do I owe you?"

"Not a thing but the fudge you make tomorrow."

"You drive a hard bargain, Logan Redmond. But I'm perfectly capable of paying you for all these beautiful Christmas items."

"It's a gift from me to you."

Revé knew that one family rental business didn't

make a man wealthy by any stretch of the imagination. Especially in a smaller-sized town. They probably barely earned a dime per item over the store's overhead after paying rent and their employees.

"Okay," she finally relented. "Fudge and cookies are the least I can do."

"I'd love your company some time," Logan said. "Dinner maybe one evening?"

"Logan—" Revé paused. "It's not practical. We're—" she shook her head. It was too awkward to speak the words of their vastly different lives, not to mention that she lived in a different state altogether.

His voice grew softer. "Now that's bad luck at the holidays. I can't even get a date with the most beautiful woman in town."

"You're incorrigible," she told him with a grin. Logan was probably the most handsome man in the entire state of New Mexico. Maybe California, too. And here she was pushing him away. But what could she do? Find herself in another impossible romantic situation? It was better not to even begin only to end up in heartache all over again.

"I'll bet you miss your family," he said now. "So I wanted to give you a little New Mexican Christmas. I'm sure you're a little homesick and missing your time with Carmen, too."

She bit her lips and gave a small nod. He was thoughtful, too, recognizing her needs and hurts.

Revé did miss her family, but she was fine without them—for the moment. Right now, it was better for her not to be pressed for information about her love life every five minutes, or have to explain why the men in her life kept leaving her. But she did miss her little nieces and nephews who probably didn't understand why Auntie Revé wasn't there for Christmas.

"What are you thinking right now?" Logan asked. "I can see a whole lot of interesting thoughts crossing your face."

She shook her head, shrugging again. "Just guilt at not going with my family. I'm a bit sad not being around all the little cousins. Christmas morning is super fun with kids in the house, but I'm not sure I'll ever have any of my own."

Logan frowned and gave her a baffled look. "Of course, you will. You're too beautiful and smart and amazing not to. You just have to find the right guy."

Her laugh was sharper than she intended. "Easier said than done."

His voice grew lower, getting almost rough and sexy, and the tingles in Revé's body grew by ten thousand percent. "I . . . have a feeling something recently happened to you in the dating department, am I right?"

She glanced away, emotion stinging the back of her eyes, as if they were betraying her. "Does it show that much?"

Revé could see flecks of darker blue color in the

center of Logan's mesmerizing eyes. Her eyes dropped to his perfectly amazing lips and then she blushed, fumbling a hand behind her to find a chair to plop into before she fell over from his hypnotic presence.

The next instant, Logan reached out to take Revé's hand in his, bursts of fireworks shooting through her chest at the touch of his skin on hers. "Hey, come over here and sit down. You've been standing a long time directing us and setting up, and you look as if you're about to fall over."

Revé's legs *were* wobbly, but not for the reasons he assumed. Nodding silently, she sank into the couch and grabbed a throw pillow to hug to her chest. Better than launching herself into his arms. She was dying to know what it felt like to melt into his arms, to feel his muscles holding her against his broad chest. But she *had* to stop these insane thoughts.

Logan Redmond was making a mess out of her. This was more than rebound after conniving, lying Warren. No man she had ever dated in her life had caused this kind of effect on her.

When she glanced up, he was sitting even closer to her. "Tell me, Revé," he said, his voice like a soothing caress. "I want to know what's going on in your mind. Carmen alluded to something, that's why you came out here, but she zipped her lips good."

Revé gave a small, self-conscious laugh. "Logan, it's tough to talk about. To admit how stupid I was. To process another betrayal. Although I'm better than I was two weeks ago."

"Why do you think that is?"

She lowered her eyes when his scrutiny overcame her. "Because," she answered, trying to be nonchalant. "Taos is a great place. I needed a change of scenery and some rest. Work's been good, but frantic, too. My family in India can be very stifling, so I confess that I'm actually running away a little bit."

Logan reached out to brush the back of his hand along her cheek. "Keep going," he said softly. "I have a feeling that this is more than a busy work schedule and family shenanigans."

Revé growled in her throat. "How'd you get to be so intuitive?"

"Because . . . I have to admit that I felt a connection with you right away," he answered, his warm hand sliding down her arm to catch her fingers in his.

Revé knew she should pull away, but his palm against her skin set her on fire. A heat she wanted to hold close and tight when he laced his fingers with hers. And yet he was a blaze that was so very dangerous, too.

She lifted her chin. "You must be a lawyer in disguise, dragging the truth out of me against my will."

"I'm a lawyer incognito," he chuckled. "Actually, I did attend law school, took the bar, but the profession is a rat race with all the rats eating each other. Dad was sick at the time, so I came home, and soon the rental business took over my life. But I like people. Maybe I'm a salesman at heart—but on my own terms."

"Law school, huh? Where did you attend?"

"UCLA," he said, his lips quirking upward.

"But that's Los Angeles! I guess you're not such a small-town cowboy that I've been assuming."

"We all have our little secrets. Now finish telling me yours, and I promise you'll feel much better when it's out of your mind for good. Because that's where things go once you've finally told someone. The bad memories fade and disappear, and the heartache will disappear with it."

She laughed out loud. "Are you now going to tell me that you're a licensed therapist?"

He chuckled with her and sank deeper into the sofa, their thighs brushing. "Well, no, but I've done a bit of counseling on a volunteer basis. I'm actually involved with the foster care system in our country. Since I'm not married, I don't personally foster any of the kids, but I do Big Brother stuff. Talk to them, do homework, play games, coach baseball."

"Oh, that's all. You should get married and have some kids of your own. You sound like you'd be an amazing father."

"That's one of my eventual goals," Logan said slowly, studying her thoughtfully. "Now, no more stalling, my gorgeous Revé."

His words made her shoot her eyes up at him again.

What had he called her? "You don't give up, do you?" she said, the words catching in her throat.

"Nope," he told her.

"Okay, okay." Revé snatched her phone from off the coffee table and brought up the video from The Markus restaurant. "If you insist, this explains it better than anything I could say. Besides, I might just lose it again and say some things I'll regret."

A confused kind of bewilderment crossed Logan's face as Revé pressed the play button, starting the video of Warren and the proposal to his new fiancé in the restaurant. While he watched, an array of emotions crossed Logan's face. Confusion, then shock, and finally outrage.

"Are you telling me that this guy—he was your old boyfriend?"

Revé's voice shook even as she fought to keep her composure. "This was barely two weeks ago. I was at a dinner meeting with some clients—the board of directors from a local hospital. Bad timing, huh? I stupidly thought—this guy—was coming over later that night to propose to *me.* What a fool I was. Blind and so stupid. One of the worst nights of my life while I had to pretend to be sane in front of the hospital president—even as I was screaming inside."

Logan pressed his lips together, a stunned expression on his face. "That jerk is a con man. A lying, conniving— well, I won't say what I'm really thinking. So . . ." Logan took a deep breath as if fearing to ask. "Do you still miss him, or think about him?"

"Surprisingly, my anger only lasted about twenty-four hours, and then I realized the man wasn't worth a single tear, so I stopped and almost never think about it now, other than to keep the evidence in hand in case I need it. Although I can't wait to erase if forever. I only saved it to show Carmen when I got here."

Logan gave her a curious look. "So what did you do at the restaurant? I can't imagine not confronting the jerk."

"Um, well, yeah, I sort of confronted him. By pouring a pitcher of ice water all over his brand-new suit—including the blonde."

Logan burst out with laughter, shaking her head. "You are a brave, feisty woman!'

"Yeah, well, I've never done anything like that before. Two days later I was on a plane to New Mexico and eating sopapillas and honey with Carmen—and you at the plaza." A blush crept up Revé's neck. "And ever since, I've been too busy recovering from snowball fights . . . and meeting a man who's nicer than I ever imagined a member of the male species could be."

"I like that part of the story," Logan said, taking one of Revé's long, dark curls in his fingers while he continued to gaze at her.

She could barely speak. "My real problem is that I

don't trust my judgment. I probably don't know my own mind. I certainly keep choosing unwisely."

"And now you doubt yourself."

"In spades," Revé admitted ruefully.

"Which means you're doubting the vibes going on between us right now," Logan added in a low voice.

Revé shook her head, pressing her fingers against her eyes. "No, I *can't* feel these vibes. I need to stop myself because they can't be real. Every relationship always goes bad in the end."

"They feel pretty real to me," Logan told her, his voice quiet and irresistible. "I was hoping I wasn't the only one feeling them."

"We shouldn't even go there. It's impossible." Revé stood up, staggering a little to regain her balance after his nearness. "You have been amazingly generous to me. I can't thank you enough. The house is going to look fantastic after I finish decorating it and all the fairy lights are glowing in the windows. Please thank your father. I'll make a plate of goodies and deliver them to him. I hope you and your family have a very Merry Christmas."

His eyes never left her face. "Just like that, you're kicking me out?"

She chewed on her lips, her voice turning raspy with sudden emotion. "I don't think you want a girl on the rebound."

"You underestimate me, Revé. I was just hoping to

hang a few ornaments, that's all," Logan said with a sly grin.

"Oh, that's all, huh?" she couldn't help retorting as a small laugh rose up her throat.

Logan shook his head. "You shouldn't be in this house alone for the next two weeks. I'll have to send over some of the kids I know to throw snowballs at your front door."

"I figured you'd say something like that. Sounds like I'll be baking cookie plates for the next week."

"Hey, there are worse things," he told her gently.

"Maybe someday I'll have a house full of kids who yell and wrestle and rip open presents and never use a napkin at the dinner table, but at the moment it doesn't look like that's in my future."

Logan gave her a slow, wicked smile.

"Stop that grinning!" she ordered. "You don't have to send over the entire foster care system!" she added, knowing what he was thinking.

Logan finally rose from the sofa and opened a box of the smaller red and gold ornaments, hanging them up on the top third of the tree where he could easily reach.

"There's your first tree ornaments," he said with another smile. "Your Taos Christmas has officially begun."

CHAPTER 14

"*Y*ou *rented* Christmas?" Carmen's exclamation came through the phone loud and clear. "Like rented the entire thing, a tree and the works?"

"Why not?" Revé said, touching one of the green glittery ornaments hanging on her beautiful Christmas tree.

"That's priceless, I love it. Who else but Revé Chatham would think about renting Christmas?" Carmen gave a laugh and then lowered her voice, hospital noises muffled in the background. "The part I like best? Logan Redmond *bringing* you Christmas. Personally delivered to the house. And he sets it up and acts like he does this all the time for his customers. Well, let me tell you he doesn't rent out decorations and he's never done anything like this for *any* other woman before. So there."

Revé twirled a piece of her long hair nonchalantly. "So there what?"

"Are you dense?" Carmen burst out. "The guy must be crazy about you. You have certainly impressed that small-town country boy."

"It was a very nice gesture," Revé said lamely, still daydreaming about Logan's warm big hand sliding down her own arm the previous night, his fingers tenderly touching hers, that devastating smile on his lips.

"Gesture? Call it the most romantic thing *ever*. He's taken with you big time."

Plopped into one of the big armchairs near the fire, Revé studied the yellow flames flickering on the dark windows. The outside of the house was ablaze with Christmas lights now, too.

Turned out Logan's hired guys had strung electric lights on the eves of the house, including wrapping them around all the shrubbery and lamp posts. It was a winter wonderland all over the entire property now.

"It's true that no other man I've ever dated before has done something like this for me," Revé admitted. "*But* Logan and I aren't dating. Not by a long shot."

"What do you call going up into the mountains and chopping down your tree? What do you call a snowball fight, and then bringing you Christmas of all the crazy things? Heck, I was surprised when he sat down a week ago at our restaurant table and ate sopapillas with us, and then wandered the plaza with us. Normally, he would have said hello, chatted for a minute, and continued on with his evening. That's what most casual, neighborhood *friends* do, honey. Don't forget that he danced with you that night, too!"

A laugh burst from Revé's throat. "Guess I'm ignorant about a lot of things."

"You need to get out of the office more," Carmen advised. "Live your life."

"I'll be thirty-four next year," Revé said wistfully. "But Logan is an impossible choice for a romantic interest. I'm leaving after New Year's. We live completely different lives. I've told him that already—the day we got the pine tree. What's a billionaire girl from a big-city-high-rise-office life and a small-town cowboy with a monster truck doing home deliveries got in common? At least not for the long term."

Carmen gave a harrumph. "There's more to life than work, honey. There's emotional connection, attraction, true honesty and goodness and hard work in a real man. And Logan has all of that in spades."

Revé chewed her lower lip. "Long distance is just too hard. I'm trying not to be stupid about this and fall hard again for another man who lives eight hundred miles away."

Even though Logan did things to Revé's heart and soul that no other man had ever done—and within just a mere week, too—a relationship just wasn't realistic.

"Wow, you're a killjoy. That didn't stop him from finding excuses to see you, to do the nicest thing *ever.*"

"I need to find a way to pay for all this Christmas stuff," Revé went on, trying to ignore her heart fluttering against her rib cage. "I feel bad that he can't return it to whatever store he got it from. Not after it's been opened and used. He had to have spent hundreds of dollars, probably more than a thousand."

"Um, Revé," Carmen said, the tone of her voice turning funny. "Honestly . . . Logan can afford it."

Revé was skeptical. "I'll bet he and his dad barely make payroll every two weeks."

Carmen let out a huge sigh. "Okay. It's not my place to tell you this, but I can't let you continue on with your misperceptions, so stop making money an excuse to run away for just one single minute."

Revé frowned at the phone. "Wow, okay. What in the world are you talking about?"

"I don't think Logan knows about your family's success this past several years, but he wouldn't care anyway. None of that matters since he gives so much of his own money away and he's so down-to-earth and *real.* Honestly, no girl could do better than Logan Redmond. And if I had to choose one of my girlfriends to end up with the guy, I'd choose *you* hands down."

"He does make my heart go full on tilt-a-whirl," Revé finally said, letting out a self-conscious laugh. "From the moment I met him, actually."

"I knew it, I knew it!" Carmen burst out. "I felt those vibes between you two right away."

"Maybe I'm just heartbroken and lonely."

"Oh, stop it!"

"Wait a minute . . ." Revé said slowly. "What did you mean when you said a moment ago that Logan doesn't care about money since he gives so much of his away?"

"Are you ready for this, girlfriend?" Carmen asked. "Logan actually owns a dozen or more rental shops all over the country. He started the business, his dad just helps him out after he retired from Los Alamos labs. Logan is whip-smart, but didn't want to sit in an office or practice law in a courtroom. He's adventurous, so when his rental company turned so successful, he figured he'd open up a bunch of locations. Now he travels the country visiting them and running them with his managers. The guy is worth probably a few tens of millions of dollars by now, if not hundreds of the seven zero digits. I don't know for sure, of course," Carmen added with a snort of laughter. "He's never told me *all* the details of his life."

Revé felt like she'd just been hit by a brick. "You're telling me that Logan is actually a rich man?"

"Yep. Mr. Redmond is filthy rich, but he donates to everything. He's a regular—what's that word that you call people who sit on charity boards and opens things like hospitals and university buildings?"

"A philanthropist," Revé said automatically while her

brain whirred trying to take in everything Carmen had just told her.

Logan was an even better man than she already knew. Was there actually a possibility for the two of them? It was a crazy, mind-blowing, and astonishing thought, but hope flared inside of her and she knew it was true.

CHAPTER 15

Revé spent the final few days before Christmas touring Taos' historical sites—and baking up a storm. She'd never had so much practice.

Baking was something she'd done with her mother as a child, but once her father's fledgling pharmaceutical company took off she rarely spent time in the kitchen. Instead they ordered out, used catering companies for holiday events, and finally, her mother hired a cook.

When Revé got her own apartment, it was easier to microwave or grab something on the way home—or eat at the office at her desk. She was having a lovely time living in an actual house with big rooms and gorgeous views—and a superlative kitchen.

Revé made a colossal mess, spilled flour and sugar, went through three aprons, but it was gratifying to see the various cookies and bars and fudge and caramels turn out so lovely.

Then she cut and wrapped them up, trudging the neighborhood to deliver and wish the folks living in the hilly neighborhood a Merry Christmas.

On Christmas Eve, she loaded up the car with twenty plates all wrapped in red cellophane and attached with gold and green bows and drove to Redmond's Rentals.

Logan must have spotted her through the windows because he immediately came out to meet her in the parking lot. "Revé, what are you doing out here?"

"Should I not have come?" she said, widening her eyes at his apparent surprise.

Logan's face broke into a huge smile, his blue eyes flashing under the cold, but sunny day. "Of course not, I'm just so happy to see you."

"You've been scarce the past several days," Revé found herself saying.

"I got worried that I was scaring you off," he admitted. "Coming on too strong."

"I know," she said, her voice barely a whisper. "I was scared. I've had so much bad luck—"

"More than your share, and what that last jerk did to you was so wrong on a hundred different levels. Unforgivable to break a woman's heart like that. Not to mention, cowardly and gutless."

Revé's heart thumped hard, and her stomach shot up into her throat when Logan reached out to take her mittened hand in his, bringing it to his lips for a quick kiss and sending ripples of fire through her despite the gloves covering her skin.

"But you're a survivor, too, despite a broken heart," Logan went on. "I want to try to erase those scars if you'll let me. Not just heal them. Erase them for good."

She was hoping he could—he seemed like the man who could—but she was also scared to dream. "I think we can see what happens," she finally said. "Especially when I learned some secrets about you from Carmen, Mr. Logan Redmond."

"Carmen spilled all of my secrets, huh? That girl," he chuckled. "I'm an open book, Revé. Ask me anything. I'll never deceive you."

"I'll take you up on that," she told him. "But for now, maybe I'm not as worried about trying to see a man who lives so far away when it appears as though he'll be in California quite a bit for his own work. I travel to our labs, too, so if you're ever in Chicago or Atlanta, we could have dinner."

"Revé, I want more than just dinner once every few months," Logan said. "And yes, I'm in Los Angeles and various other cities a few times a month." His lips quirked up. "I have this nice little contraption called a private plane. It even comes with a pilot—me."

Staggering back a step, Revé let out her breath. "So, Carmen *wasn't* exaggerating about you."

"Sorry, but I try to hide the filthy lucre as best as I

can. Can I stop by later? We're closing early for Christmas Eve."

A shot of adrenaline went through Revé. "Sure, what would you like for dinner? I'll even cook."

"You're not sick of being in the kitchen? From the look of those goodie plates on the back seat, you must be dead on your feet."

"Not too much, and a nice quiet Christmas Eve dinner sounds good. You can help me set up the luminarias, too."

He let out a gust of laughter. "Oh, you have ulterior motives, huh! That's why I get invited to dinner."

Revé cocked her head at him demurely. "Well, it'll be fun, right?"

"It will be wonderful, just you wait. Now let me help you carry those cookie plates inside."

"I wanted to thank your father and your crew for making my Christmas and my time here in New Mexico so special."

"I knew you were a keeper," he teased.

"Compliments will only get you so far, buddy," she shot back.

"But I can try," he told her, grinning broadly.

The gift plates were carefully balanced in two boxes so between the two of them they carried them inside the warehouse where most of the staff were drinking cider and chatting and laughing.

The interior of the store was nearly empty now, most people home and cooking for Christmas Eve.

There were exclamations of delight from Logan's staff when they saw the plates, especially from the single men.

His eyes drooling at the sight of the beautiful array of sweets, Keith Redmond thanked Revé and put a quick fatherly arm around her shoulders. "I volunteered to stay on for any last-minute renters after we release the staff. This'll be my dinner tonight."

"Just don't go into a sugar coma," Revé warned him.

He winked at her. "I'll call my wife to bring pizza and keep me company."

It was nice to see that Logan had great parents, that's probably what made him such a generous and giving person.

Now she had butterflies in her stomach at the thought of dinner with the man. She needed to make one last quick trip to the grocery store on the way back to the Hurley home.

Asking advice from grocery manager, Revé learned that tamales, salsa, rice, beans, and sopapillas was the traditional Christmas Eve dinner. Most people made their own tamales, quite an all-day process it seemed, but the store had some good ones in the deli section.

Revé also purchased three white tapered candles to light for the table. Dessert was a no-brainer since she had enough dessert to last another week!

Hurrying home, she made sure the house was in order, all the Christmas lights were going full blast inside and out, and then set to work steaming the tamales and setting a pot of rice to simmer.

When the doorbell rang, Revé was ready for him. Logan looked fantastic in jeans and a dark blue pullover sweater. He held out some hot-house yellow roses and white daisies in a bouquet of baby's breath, two red orchids perched in the very center.

"Wow, they're gorgeous, Logan, thank you," she said, breathing in the heady perfumed scent. "You have good taste, too."

"For the dinner table," he added, setting the flowers down on the dining room table before suddenly moving forward to wrap his arms around her.

The embrace caught Revé's breath. It was natural but unexpected, and her heart was pounding in her throat at the thrill of his arms around her, enveloping her in the best hug she'd probably ever had.

It was the first time Logan had embraced her, the first time their bodies had been so close, and Revé wanted to melt into the floor as she slowly slid her arms around his neck to hug him in return.

Logan felt even more muscular and solid than he looked, and his aftershave was heavenly, a citrusy musk that made Revé's head spin.

Placing his palm on the back of her head while they held the embrace, Logan whispered in her ear. "I have a little surprise waiting in the car. Do you mind some extra dinner guests tonight?"

Revé blinked. "No, of course not. Your parents?"

"No," he answered with a smile. "They're spending Christmas Eve with my sister and her brood tonight." Sudden moisture rose in his eyes, and Revé stepped back to stare at him while he continued to hold her hands in his.

"Has something happened?" she asked, squeezing his fingers.

"No, something good. I just didn't want to spring three kids on you at the last minute."

"Three kids—as in children? Live children?"

His flustered laughter followed by a boyish grin sent a thrill up her neck. "They're real and very much alive. Three kiddos I've been helping in the foster program. They're siblings, and the family they were supposed to spend Christmas with had a sudden trip out of state. So, I volunteered."

"The children are in your truck right now?" When Logan nodded, she quickly said, "They must be freezing, go get them!"

"Oh, Revé, you're the best," Logan said, leaning down to give her a quick kiss on her cheek.

Sixty seconds later, a tall, skinny boy of about fourteen crossed the threshold with halting steps, followed by his two younger sisters who were holding hands. Their eyes grew big as saucers at the sight of the fancy decorated house and the expansive picture windows that showed off all the outdoor lights in a spectacular fashion.

"Hello, hello!" Revé said, opening the door wider. "Merry Christmas! Are you starving and ready to eat? Because I am and the food is ready!"

It didn't take long to get coats and mufflers shed and hanging on the coat rack.

"This is Max, he's almost fifteen," Logan said, introducing the group. "And this is Sarah and Lily, ten and eight respectively."

The older brother had serious gray eyes and a sober expression while his sisters were adorable with long dark hair, big brown eyes, and smiles that were sweet enough to break Revé's heart.

"I'm so happy to meet you Max and Sarah and Lily," Revé told them, giving them each a quick hug. "Come in by the fire and get warm. Your cheeks are like ice!"

While the three siblings held out their hands in front of the fireplace grate, Logan slipped an arm around Revé's waist, murmuring. "You're amazing, you know that? Let's eat."

She bent her neck to look up at him. "So are you. Help me put the food on the table, *Dad*."

"Okay, that was uncalled for," he laughed out loud. "But you have to admit, it's kind of fun, too, and these kids are so great and polite. Can we spend Christmas week with you, Revé?" he asked next, his voice lowering as he brushed his chin against her cheek and hair.

She gave a small laugh. "What does that mean?"

"I told the kids we'd go sledding and make a snowman. And, um, play games, eat popcorn, watch movies. I also have gifts for them to open in the morning."

Tears burned at Revé's eyes. "You're going to make me cry. They have nothing—nobody?" she whispered up at him.

Logan shook his head, his expression sober. "They lost their mom in a car accident about two years ago and their dad kind of lost his mind. First his job, and then his sanity. He's in a drug rehab facility up north and suffering major depression. We're trying to find a family that can take them for the rest of the school year until their father gets out. Extended family is sparse and unable to take them."

"Can I take them home with me?" Revé said with a small, wistful sigh. "They're beautiful children, and they seem so sweet. What a devastating time they've had losing both their parents in such difficult circumstances."

"The foster care system is struggling to find answers to it all. Meanwhile, we can give them a great Christmas to remember," Logan said with a soft smile.

Revé nodded, gazing into the man's kind and empathetic face. What a good man he was, and with every passing day, she was getting more and more attached to

Logan Redmond. A tantalizing, but potentially dangerous outcome if she wasn't careful.

After eating an early dinner, dusk was beginning to settle, and everyone pitched in to get the luminarias put together.

Max filled the bags with two scoops of sand, the girls placed the candles, and Revé and Logan positioned them up and down the driveway, the fence line and the raised flower beds. Then Logan used the long lighters to get the candles lit, Max especially eager to help with that part.

While a bright moon rose slowly above the mountains, the luminarias glowed a beautiful golden yellow in the chilly, dark night.

Sarah and Lilly clapped their hands in delight.

"Aren't they so *beautiful*," Revé said, putting an arm around the girls.

They snuggled up close to her and Sarah said, "Our Mom used to say that the luminarias lit the path for the Christ Child to find us on Christmas Eve and bless all the families."

"Your mother was exactly right," Revé said. "What a beautiful night to be born. We're going to drive around the neighborhood to see all the Christmas lights, and then we're going to head into the plaza to see the thousands of luminarias at the church. But later when we get back home, I want you to tell me all about your mama, okay?"

Lily nodded, slipping her hand into Revé's and squeezing tight.

"Don't you think the kids should spend the night here, too, Logan?" she asked quietly. "After all, tomorrow is Christmas morning, and they'll need to open their presents."

"You read my mind," he said, gazing at Revé in wonderment. "We actually had a lot of donations, and there are new pajamas and presents in the truck for them. They'll love staying here instead of my stark bachelor pad."

"The Hurley house has a few empty bedrooms. It will only take ten minutes to change the sheets."

"A slumber party!" Lily said, clapping her hands.

"Slumber parties are the best," Revé agreed, laughing. "I haven't been to one since I was about thirteen. So, I'm long overdue. Maybe we need sleeping bags and lots of blankets for cuddling, too."

Logan jumped in. "I'll bet I can rustle up a few sleeping bags from the Hurley garage. We'll lay them out on the living room floor in front of the fire for when we come back after our trip into town. I think some hot cocoa will be on the menu about that time."

"And I'll dig out some extra snuggly blankets from the linen closets," Revé added. "I think we need to do a movie and popcorn night, too."

"Yes, yes," Sarah cried. "Doesn't that sound like fun, Max?"

Her brother gave a slow smile and shrugged. "Whatever you want, Sarah."

"I'll bring in the gifts right now," Logan said, heading to his truck.

"I'll help you, Logan," Max said, hurrying after him.

Revé smiled to herself as she watched the two of them together. A young man like Max needed someone like Logan in his life. What a sad situation, but Christmas always made life brighter for a little wedge of time and gave people *hope*. What would the world be like without the generosity of people like Logan Redmond who brought life and laughter everywhere he went?

CHAPTER 16

An hour later, all five of them were stuffed into Logan's truck and arriving at the plaza. The place was alive with people on foot perusing through the square or heading down to the Taos church for Christmas Eve Mass.

Tramping through a light dusting of snow, Logan led them on a tour of the town's luminaria spectacle, and each of the children gasped in awe at the wonderment of the thousands of lights glowing a luminescent yellow in the dark night air.

"Its like a fairyland," Lily whispered, holding tight onto Revé's hand and not letting her go.

A peaceful quiet reigned amidst the beauty of it all, the only sound the soft shushing of boots and the whispers of people as they wandered the plaza with all of its nooks and crannies and little shops.

"I'm awestruck," Revé whispered, tucking her free hand into Logan's arm. "I've never seen anything quite like it. There must be *thousands* of luminarias."

"I'm awestruck, too," he said with a meaningful smile as he reached over to straighten the knitted cap pulled over her head with a small tug.

"Out there, Logan," she said, lifting an eyebrow. "I'm awestruck over *the lights* and all the thousands of candles glowing. It's peaceful and inspiring, and absolutely magical."

He continued to gaze at her while he placed an arm around her shoulders to bring her in closer to his side. "I don't need to look anywhere else for the most beautiful sight in the world."

"You are too flattering, Logan Redmond."

"I mean every word I say," he told her in his deep, quiet voice.

Revé shook her head, even as she grinned back at him. "I'm beginning to suspect that you might have quite a romantic heart, Logan Redmond."

When the kid's teeth began to chatter, they headed back to the house, Logan's truck easily climbing the slippery roads. Once inside the house, coats and scarves were flung across the couches while Max and Logan spread out cushy sleeping bags on the floor in front of the fireplace.

While Logan showed Max how to build and light the fire, Revé made popcorn and hot cocoa with Sarah and Lily in the kitchen. "We worked up an appetite after all that walking," she said. "Are you sure we had dinner?"

Lily giggled. "I had two tamales!"

"Me, too," Sarah added. "The sopapillas were yummy, too, Miss Chatham."

"Please call me Revé, sweetie. Today was my first time ever making sopapillas, and they didn't turn out too bad if I do say so myself. The honey really helps on the almost burned parts though," she added with silly laugh. "I think tomorrow we need to make cut-out sugar cookies and frost and decorate them—after we open our presents!"

"There are presents!?" the two sisters exclaimed, their eyes widening with excitement.

"If I'm not mistaken, this is the night Santa Claus comes," Logan called out from the great room. He reached over to switch off the table lamps so the room glowed with only the Christmas tree lights reflecting off the windows that overlooked the front yard.

"What movie should we watch?" Max asked.

"*Rudolph the Red-nosed Reindeer!*" his sisters chorused.

"Sounds great," Logan agreed. "But hand over some of that popcorn."

"We'll just make more," Revé told him, punching him lightly on the arm.

Without hesitation, Logan caught her hand, entwining their fingers in a warm, close clasp. He leaned in, his eyes riveted to hers. "I've been waiting a long time to properly hold your hand, you know."

"Is that so?" she asked, a thrill rising in her stomach at the touch of his skin against hers. "But I do have a request. After *Rudolph* is over, I propose that we watch my favorite movie, *The Princess Bride*."

Logan let out a low whistle. "Wow, that's a blast from the past. I haven't seen that since I was a kid."

Before they could find the movie on the shelf of DVD's, Christmas carolers arrived at the front door.

Logan quickly gathered the three children together and the five of them stood there, cold air from the open door whooshing through the room while they listened to *Joy to the World* and *We Wish You a Merry Christmas* followed by the sweet and peaceful *Silent Night*.

"Merry Christmas!" The group of singers called out as they continued on to the next house down the road.

"It's a perfect Christmas," Sarah said, moving close to Revé while Lily took her other side.

She put an arm around the girls and squeezed them close, brushing a quick kiss against their hair. "It *is* a perfect Christmas. Now jump into your jammies and get ready to laugh a lot."

Two hours later, *The Princess Bride* was nearing the end, and the kids had giggled over Miracle Max and his funny wife, while every time Vizzini blurted out, "Inconceivable!" just before he fell over from the poison, they rolled with giggles.

The girls loved the romance of Westley and Buttercup and sighed happily when the pair of lovers finally found each other again after so many years.

Max enjoyed the thrilling scenes of Westley dueling swords with Inigo Montoya, and then they all cheered when the king and his horrible general were tied up at last so that Westley and Buttercup and their cohorts could escape out the castle window on four white horses.

The kids were falling asleep by then, exhausted after all the evening's activities. It was nearly midnight now.

Logan carried the girls to their beds in the guest rooms, the two sisters sharing a big double-sized bed while Max staggered sleepily into his own room.

Tucking them in, Revé's heart was so full she thought it would burst. "I think this may be my most favorite Christmas ever."

Logan pulled her against him and whispered in her ear. "I like hearing that. I hope we have many more Christmases together."

"Why does it feel like I've known you longer than ten days?" she asked, gazing up at him.

"You mean you're not still pining after Warren?" he replied, pretending to be shocked.

Revé gave him a sly smile. "Who is this Warren you speak of? I haven't the faintest idea who you're talking about."

Logan chuckled and said. "Go grab your coat and hat

and gloves. We're going to head outside for one last look at the world."

"Seriously? It must be ten degrees out there by now."

"Just do it. Five minutes. You'll love it."

"Okay, okay, I'll freeze out there, but you're on," Revé finally said as Logan tugged her by the hand toward the front door and the coat rack.

After shoving her feet back into her boots, Revé pulled on her winter coat, knitted hat, and gloves. Logan wrapped a thick muffler around her neck, then tucked his gloved hand into hers.

She followed obediently while Logan opened the front door and then led her outside into a winter wonderland.

CHAPTER 17

The world was quiet and still. Soft and magical.

Holding her hand, Logan led Revé down the curving stone pathways around the perimeter of the yard. Snow crunched under their feet, an odd sound in a world that was so quiet it almost felt like nobody else existed but the two of them.

Stars glittered like diamonds had been thrown against the dark blue of the sky while the mountains surrounding them were silent shadows in the glow of a perfect white moon.

While she stared up at the heavens, cold air bit at Revé's cheeks and her breath blew out like a stream of smoke, but it seemed like she had stepped through a doorway into an entirely new world of unspeakable beauty.

"It's pure enchantment out here, Logan," she whispered, slipping her arm through his elbow while they leaned in to one another.

"It's something else," he agreed. "Christmas Eve might be my favorite night of the year."

"I can see why. I've heard Carmen talk about it before, but I had no idea how special it is to see it in person. This must be one of the reasons they call New Mexico the Land of Enchantment."

"Soon you'll be a native," Logan teased. "Frying your own sopapillas, baking biscochitos and bread in an outdoor *horno*."

"And what, pray tell, is an *horno*?"

"A rounded outdoor oven made out of adobe in your backyard. You build a fire inside from stacks of wood until it burns down to coals, then slide in your food and let it slow cook or bake. Perfection. *Spanish hornos* go back hundreds of years."

"Will you make me my very own *horno*, then, Mr. Redmond?" Revé laughed and the sound of her voice carried across the quiet neighborhood, even if the neighbors were all a quarter of a mile away scattered about the foothills of the mountains.

"I'll make you a dozen if you'd like," he said, softly chuckling.

Holding hands, they circled the pathways around the house while the hundreds of luminaries they'd set up earlier glowed a warm gold and yellow as the small candles flickered inside the brown paper bags.

Soft, pristine snow lay in drifts along the shrubbery and hedges, lit up by the same moon that cast a silvery light over the world.

"Are you too cold yet?" Logan finally asked. He took off a glove to place a warm palm against Revé's cheeks and she found herself leaning into his hand and closing her eyes for a moment. "Yep, those cheeks of yours are pretty chilled."

"Your hands feel wonderful. Like a fire." She took off his other glove and pressed both his hands to her face. "Okay, just stay right there and I'll be fine."

"I'm your personal hand-warmer, huh?"

She gave him a sly grin. "Something like that."

There was a moment of silence while Logan gazed at her. Then, slowly, he leaned in to softly kiss her face before taking her in his arms for a warm embrace.

Revé let out the breath she'd been holding. Was this moment really happening? Her heart was about to fly right out of her chest. She didn't think anything was more perfect than being in his arms. But it was mighty frigid out here.

Finally, she stepped back. "As beautiful as it is out here, I'm about to turn into a popsicle."

"I agree, let's go back inside."

"Race you to the front door!"

"Don't slip on the ice!" Logan warned.

They both reached the double doors at the same time. After Revé tagged it with her hand, she turned to gaze out at the lights of Christmas Eve one last time, sighing with the utter beauty that it was.

"Being here—seeing this for myself—honestly feels like anything could happen. Like the world is filled with the possibilities of anything. Of true magic."

"Hey, let's go check on the kiddos once more. Make sure none of them got up and went looking for us."

"That would be terrible, especially in a strange house."

Logan opened the front door and Revé scurried inside, stripping off her heavy winter coat and gloves to race toward the warm fire. "This feels *perfect*. Oh, blessed heat."

When he took her hand to tiptoe into the bedrooms for a final peek at the sleeping children, Revé allowed herself to be pulled along behind him, her stomach in her throat.

This man was amazing. Dare she hope there could be something more? Was it too soon? She'd never thought it was possible to fall for a man so quickly, so easily. She'd heard of it happening to people but always scoffed at the idea of it.

"Okay, quiet," Logan whispered, checking on Max first. The boy was spread-eagle on the bed, blankets askew, but snoring softly. "I swear he's getting taller every time I lay eyes on the him."

Lily and Sarah were sleeping quietly, curled up into balls under their blankets, their dark hair spread like angel wings against their pillows.

"They're beautiful children," Revé said wistfully. "They deserve a good home and family."

"Whenever I'm around them—and even when I'm not—I want to adopt them," Logan agreed. "And then I want some kids of my own. Maybe I can make that happen. Somehow. I really need to look into trying to become their foster Dad again. Perhaps a family court judge would look at more than my single status. The kids sometimes bring it up and it breaks my heart."

"Maybe you'll soon find the right woman to make it happen. With these children. And maybe some of your own one day," Revé whispered, daring to speak the words she'd been feeling all day—and hoping Logan wouldn't turn around and run straight for the front door.

"She may be closer than I ever imagined," Logan whispered in return, taking her hand to return to the warm living room. "Hey, let's watch the last part of the movie one more time."

"You're on," Revé told him. After taking the movie back about fifteen minutes, she set down the remote just as Logan laced her fingers with his once again. A crazy jump of excitement flew into her throat at his touch. How could holding hands feel so personal and intimate?

"This is such a classic," Logan said, slipping his other arm around her shoulders and pulling her tight against him.

Revé held her breath as Westley and Buttercup leaned toward each other, ever so slowly, as the movie's soundtrack soared and the narrator repeated those famous words, *"Since the invention of the kiss, there have only been five kisses that were rated the most passionate, the most pure. This one left them all behind."*

The kiss between Westley and Buttercup was romance at its finest and Revé's stomach tumbled at the idea of the most passionate kiss existing out there in the world.

A few moments later, the end-of-the film credits rolled and Logan turned to Revé. "Hey, now that the kids are asleep, is this what it feels like when you're a real parent?"

"I suspect so," she whispered back. "But I hope I can find out for real someday."

"Me, too, Revé, me too."

"You big flirt," she chided softly.

"I mean every single word, and I never lie, you can even ask my mom," he added with a low chuckle.

"Maybe I'll do just that." Laughter bubbled up Revé throat as they grinned at each other. It was like fifteen years of time suddenly disappeared and she was a teenager again. And yet, the feelings she was having for this man were more powerful than any she had ever felt before. Even the men she had allowed herself to be engaged to over the last several years. How lucky she was that those marriages had never taken place.

Logan released his hand from hers while one arm went around her waist to pull her even closer.

Sitting on her side against the sofa Revé was now facing him. Tentatively, she slid her arms up along his biceps and then around his neck, her heart beating wildly. Logan was warm and perfect and wonderful.

Could he actually be the right man for her? Was this the moment she had been waiting for her whole life?

"I'm scared," she suddenly whispered. "Scared of the future. Because of the past."

"I know," Logan told her gently. "The question is, do you believe in Christmas?"

Revé lifted her eyebrows questioningly. "Of course I do, what do you mean?"

"Well, Christmas is about healing. It's about faith and hope and new beginnings. Possibilities of a better future because of what happened that long ago Christmas night."

"Are you for real?" Revé asked, shaking her head as she stared at him. "I don't think I've ever met anyone like you."

"I like the sound of that," he teased, his voice low and sexy in the dim room while the fire crackled and the tree's lights shimmering all around them. "It goes both ways, Revé. I've never met anyone like you either. Haven't had a serious girlfriend for a very long time. Most of my relationships never got past a superficial surface."

Revé gave a short laugh. "I was the foolish one to get engaged. And then basically left at the altar twice. Do you really want a girl with that kind of a shaky past—someone who doesn't know her own mind?"

"I think you know exactly what you want. You've just never found it before," Logan said, never taking his eyes off her face.

"How did you get to be so wise, Mr. Redmond?" Revé asked with a quirky smile.

He shrugged. "Not exactly wise, but maybe I just never gave up hope. I knew there was someone out there, I just had to find her. Little did I know I'd find her on a road just as she was about to go over a cliff."

Revé laughed and gave a little punch in the arm. "Very funny. You and your big monster truck."

Those deep blue eyes penetrated right into Revé's heart. "Do you want to take a leap of faith with me? Choose the possibility of this being the real thing?"

"It—it sounds incredible. But how do I get past my broken self?"

Logan shook his head. "You're not broken, you never were. I think being here has been a healing experience. Taking time for yourself. Getting away from the rat race of L.A. and all the expectations you've put on yourself."

Revé nodded slowly. "Being around those darling children today has only fortified my desire to have a family of my own."

"Don't lose your dreams," Logan whispered, brushing a tendril of hair away from her face.

He cupped his hands behind her head and pulled her toward him so that she was leaning against his broad chest, their faces only a breath apart. Revé's entire body sizzled with desire and it felt as though a radiant light was shooting out of every strand of her hair, and every inch of her skin.

Ever so slowly, Logan leaned forward to softly press his lips against Revé's mouth in the warmest and most sensuous kiss she could have ever dreamed of.

Turning her head slightly to taste the man's warm, perfect lips more fully, Revé's stomach dropped when Logan deepened the kiss. He kissed her until she was breathless and light-headed. Her heart was about to fly straight out of her chest and launch toward the heavens.

The fire was beginning to die down, turning into a pile of glowing orange coals in the grate, but Revé's face was hot and flushed as they continued to kiss and kiss and kiss.

When Logan pulled her legs over his lap to turn her body even closer to him, tiny pin-pricks of emotion burned at Revé's eyes. Something big was happening.

This was it! The most passionate, the most beautiful kiss she had ever experienced with the most perfect man she had ever met. Just like her favorite movie's final words.

After five more minutes of an explosion of perfect kissing, Logan murmured against Revé's mouth, "Is this the kiss you've been waiting for, sweetheart?"

When he said things like that—as if he truly knew her—a powerful happiness filled her entire being. "How did you know?" she asked. "It's like you can read my mind, my heart."

A boyish grin spread across his face. "Oh, I don't know, but after watching *The Princess Bride*, it wasn't just a lucky guess."

Laughing quietly together, Logan bent to kiss her neck and then the corners of her mouth before pulling her face close to his again. His hands were warm around her body and Revé grasped his upper arms, an ache of longing rising inside of her.

Laughter combined with tears bubbled up her throat. Revé was discombobulated and overcome with love for this incredible man. Not to mention wildly and deliriously happy. She had finally had her honest-to-goodness Westley and Buttercup kiss.

"Yep, this kiss has left all the others behind," she admitted, quoting the movie. "I know what I want now," she added, pressing her mouth against those perfect lips of his, wanting more and more. Finally, she broke away in a small gasp of exhilaration.

"You are something else, Revé Chatham," Logan told her in his husky, flirtatious voice.

Hope filled Revé up like a balloon ready to fly through the ceiling to the stars. "I think I can finally stop looking because the man I want is right here in front of me. That is, if you haven't changed your mind after keeping you at arm's length for so long."

"Don't worry, I'm never going to let you go, Revé," Logan told her, running his fingers through the swirls of thick dark hair that fell around her shoulders. "The only problem is your dratted job."

"It's pretty important work, I'll have you know!" She teased, her eyes widening. "But there's always remote working with the occasional trip to Los Angeles for meetings. There are inventions now called telephones and internet and online meetings."

"Piece of cake, then. Watch out world. Revé Chatham is going to light you on fire. She's already lit my world on fire."

Revé's voice went husky, emotion welling up in her throat. "Will you promise me one thing?"

"Anything you want," he said with a teasing smile.

"Promise me that you'll kiss me like this for the rest of our lives?"

"*As you wish,*" Logan said, repeating Westley's dashing

words from the movie. "Forever and ever, my beautiful Revé."

His gaze met hers with assurance and happiness, and Revé saw everything in those deep blue eyes of Logan Redmond that she had always hoped to see in the man she wanted to spend the rest of her life with.

DEAR ROMANCE LOVER

~

I hope you enjoyed reading *The Billionaire's Christmas Hideaway!* I love writing sweet romance that sweeps me into new and wonderful worlds. Since I live in a small town in New Mexico it was super fun to write about Christmas in Taos—such a magical and historic town in the beautiful mountains of northern New Mexico.

Please check out my other romance novels on Amazon, including my *Secret Billionaire Romances.* They're all FREE on Kindle Unlimited, too.

If you'd like to be the first to hear about new releases sign up to my Reader's Club Newsletter and never miss a thing. Subscribe and receive a free book! http://eepurl. com/NBXon

xo,

~Kimberley Montpetit

P.S. Keep turning the pages to read the first chapter in THE NEIGHBOR'S SECRET and THE EXECU-TIVE'S SECRET from my *Secret Billionaire Romance* series!

~

Kimberley Montpetit once spent all her souvenir money at the *La Patisserie* shops when she was in Paris—on the arm of her adorable husband. The author grew up in San Francisco, but currently lives on a dirt road in a small town along the Rio Grande with her big, messy family.

Kimberley reads a book a day and loves to travel. She's stayed in the haunted tower room at Borthwick Castle in Scotland, sailed the Seine in Paris, ridden a camel among the glorious cliffs of Petra, shopped the maze of the Grand Bazaar in Istanbul, and spent the night in an old Communist hotel in Bulgaria.

Every time she starts writing a new book, Kimberley makes a LOT of chocolate chip cookie dough.

Find all of Kimberley's Novels on Amazon

Get FREE Books when you subscribe to Kimberley's Newsletter: http://eepurl.com/NBXon

ALSO BY KIMBERLEY MONTPETIT

A romantic & bestselling series set in Snow Valley:

Risking it all for Love

Romancing Rebecca

Sealed with a Kiss

Unbreak my Heart

The Secret of a Kiss

Love in Snow Valley, Boxed Set, Books 1-5

A Secret Billionaire Romance series has launched!

The Neighbor's Secret

The Executive's Secret

The Mafia's Secret

The Owner's Secret

The Billionaire's Christmas Hideaway

The Fiancé's Secret

A Secret Billionaire Boxed Set, Book 1 - 6

NEW SERIES!

MOSTLY DANGEROUS: The Women of Ambrose Estate, Book 1

Mostly Perilous: The Women of Ambrose Estate, Book 2

The FBI Bride, An Undercover Bridesmaid Romance, Book 1

The Undercover Bridesmaid, An Undercover Bridesmaid Romance, Book 2

Fake Fiance Romantic Suspense Series:

Her Secret Agent Fake Fiance

Her Undercover Spy Fake Fiance

Her CIA Operative Fake Husband

Her Double Life Fake Fiance

Purchase Kimberley's Books on Amazon

Keep reading for a sneak peek at the first chapters of *The Neighbor's Secret* and *The Executive's Secret,* Book 1 and Book 2 of my very popular Secret Billionaire Romance series!

Subscribe to Kimberley's Newsletter and get free books and the chance for other goodies!

http://eepurl.com/NBXon

It was the perfect day for a wedding. After months of
trying on wedding gowns, ordering invitations, and

searching every bridal boutique in Toronto for the perfect shoes, Allie Strickland was ready to walk—maybe even run—down the aisle of the church and into Sean Carter's waiting arms.

She'd licked stamps to post the more than one hundred announcements until her tongue was dry. She'd suffered through at least that many long-distance phone calls with her mother that sometimes ended in arguments and tears.

If she didn't stop weeping, Allie's mother joked, their tiny town of Heartland Cove was going to flood over. The calls and planning were finally over, and Allie's wedding day was here.

That morning she'd taken her big fat red marker and made an X on the calendar.

"Mrs. Sean Carter, here I come," she whispered as she capped the pen and tossed it inside a packing box.

During their five years of dating, she and Sean had gone through grad school together, first jobs, and now Sean was climbing the ladder to become a partner with Learner & Associates Law Firm.

Tonight she'd be with the man of her dreams forever. No more work interruptions. No more hurried lunches. No more agonizingly long street car rides to get to one another's apartments. Lately, they'd just meet somewhere for a late dinner.

Tomorrow, new renters were moving into her apartment on Bloor Street. When she and Sean returned from their honeymoon to the Bahamas, Allie would unpack the boxes sitting inside Sean's apartment and officially move in.

Allie's stomach jumped as she checked the time on her phone. Her wedding began in ninety minutes and it would take at least half of that just to get through Toronto traffic.

She sent a text to Sean and then tried to take deep breaths in an effort to settle her nerves while staring at tightly packed buildings and Roger's Stadium glinting in the late afternoon sun.

With her brother Jake at the wheel and the car full of her mother, sister, and best friend Marla on their way to the Episcopal Church, Allie's brain went over her luggage packed for fun, sun, and the beach.

Three bikinis; red, black, and purple.

Slinky dresses for candlelit dinners.

Five pairs of shoes, including a pair of running shoes.

Lingerie and toiletries.

She couldn't *wait* to get on that plane tomorrow morning and leave work and stress and family behind.

Seven perfect days with Sean. Finally, finally, finally.

"I don't think Toronto has ever looked lovelier," Allie sighed happily, pressing her nose against the window glass like a kid.

She was excited, anxious, and terrified all at once—and missing Sean. She hadn't seen him in three days due to his working overtime so he'd have a few days off for their honeymoon.

"I promise we'll have a longer honeymoon when I'm finished with this current trial," he'd said last week. "A cruise of the Greek Islands in autumn."

"You know all my dreams," she'd told him, throwing her arms around his neck and feeling the beat of his heart against hers.

Pulling her arms down, Sean had given her a peck goodbye. "You know I have to be in the courtroom at seven a.m., Allie."

She'd frowned, turning away to stare out the window of her apartment. It was a spectacular view of downtown and the lake. She'd been lucky to get this flat a year ago and hated to let it go, but Sean had a bigger place so she'd reluctantly given up her dream apartment.

"That case has taken over your life. *Our* lives," she said, trying not to whine. "We haven't been out in ages. We've hardly kissed in months."

"But we're getting married in a few days, Allie. Be a grown-up and get used to the hectic life of a criminal defense lawyer."

She despised those moments when he treated her like a child. But all she could say was, "But I *miss* you. Don't you miss me?"

As soon as she spoke the words, Allie chomped down on her tongue. Sentiments like those merely underscored his assessment of her as a petulant child.

"Your dress!" Mrs. Strickland suddenly shrieked from the front passenger seat, motioning to Jake that there was a red light before throwing a glare at her daughter in her wedding finery.

"These darn no left turn streets," Jake muttered, braking so hard they all lunged forward. "Traffic is horrible. They've got the next two streets blocked off for a 10K run."

Quickly, Allie hitched up the beaded satin wedding gown around her to prevent wrinkles on the back end.

"You simply *can't* have wrinkles when you walk down the aisle," her sister Erin said with a dose of sarcasm. "It would be, like, a crime or something."

Mrs. Strickland gave her youngest daughter a second glare and then silently held out her palm when Erin snapped her gum.

Erin stuck her wad of chewing gum in her mother's hand, smashing it down vehemently in revenge, and leaned back with a sulk.

"Thanks for the gum sacrifice," Allie told her, nudging at her sister's shoulder.

"Huh," Erin grunted, sliding another pack of spearmint contraband from her handbag.

"Look at the blue sky and enjoy the fact that there isn't ten feet of snow on the ground."

"You mean smog and obnoxiously tall concrete they call architecture."

"You only think that because you're sixteen."

"Girls!" their mother cried, craning her neck to check the name of the cross street. "Don't fight on your wedding day."

Jake remained stoic, his mobile giving out directions in an English accent.

"It's not *my* wedding day," Erin said, making one of her famous faces, eyes wide, nostrils flaring.

"Obviously. But today is Allie's most special day in her entire life. Be nice. Mind your manners. And *please* don't put your chewed gum on the dinner plate at the reception this evening."

"I'm not eight!" Erin crossed her arms over the deep maroon bridesmaid dress. Lower cut in the bust line than Mrs. Strickland had suggested, but nobody had listened to her protests when the wedding planning rose to extreme levels of tension.

Marla Perry, Allie's best friend since Kindergarten, reached over with a tissue. "You've got a smudge of frosting on your face, Allie."

"Where?" Allie scrabbled inside her white lace-covered wedding bag for a mirror, which, of course, only held two tissues and a lipstick for refreshing. Allie had a tendency to bite off her lip color. "How could you let me leave the house like that?"

"It's just a tiny smidge," Marla assured her. "Probably cream cheese from the cinnamon roll."

"You just *had* to go and make cinnamon rolls for

breakfast on the day I wanted to be my skinniest best self," Allie teased.

"I knew you'd go all day without food if I didn't give you something. And then we'd be picking you up off the floor in front of the minister when you fainted from starvation."

"Not starvation. Sugar overload. I should have had a granola bar."

"Granola bars are for birds, not real people," Marla said. "Fainting can be a means to an end. Sean could scoop you up from the cold floor and kiss you passionately."

Marla had snagged the lead role in *Romeo and Juliet* in their high school drama production class and swore she'd leave the tiny town of Heartland Cove and run away to New York City. She'd gotten as far as Toronto—which, for a Heartland Cove resident, that boasted a population of 899 was, nevertheless, a major feat. But her Fine Arts degree in photography was proving difficult to find a decent paying job.

She'd finally taken a position shooting kids school photos all over town with Life Touch, but was determined to open her own business.

The thought of having your own business was exciting. Despite using her MBA to snag a good paying position, Allie was bored to tears with financial reports and office politics as the manager at a small branch of The Royal Bank.

"Mom. Chill," Jake said at last. Miss British GPS voice told him to turn right, but when he did he hit another red light and jerked to a stop. All the women braced a hand on their seats, then adjusted dresses and jewelry.

"Warn us next time, Jake," Mrs. Strickland said, the frown deepening between her eyes.

Allie did not miss the family dynamics living in Toronto, although she sometimes got nostalgic for Heartland Cove, the town where she'd been born, worked her teen summers at the Strickland Family Fry Truck, and had her first kiss on the Bridge of Heartland Cove with a boy who told her he'd love her forever—and then promptly moved to Newfoundland three weeks later. It might as well have been Timbuktu.

After a few sexy Facebook messages, he'd posted a picture of himself with a suntanned blond girl—and disappeared from her life forever.

In Heartland Cove he'd been her only possibility for a boyfriend until she'd met Sean her senior year as an undergrad in Business School.

Sean Carter was the complete opposite of the boy from tiny Heartland Cove High. Tall, slim and dark-haired with smoldering eyes and a crooked grin that melted her heart.

"I think butterflies have set up permanent house-keeping in my stomach," Allie said, while the clock ticked down to the moment they both said, "I do".

Sean was now on the verge of being offered the position of junior partner at Learner & Associates. He'd worked hard and received top marks in law school. Now the man lived and breathed law, briefs, and depositions. He had a sharp mind and was quickly becoming a talented and incisive criminal lawyer. Being in the courtroom gave him a thrill like riding the most daring roller coaster at Six Flags.

Sometimes, Allie worried that *she* wasn't thrilling enough. The only time Sean got truly passionate was after he'd argued a heated and feisty trial.

Mrs. Strickland patted her hand. A little bit comforting. A little bit impatiently. And a little bit sadly.

"You alright Mom?" Allie asked.

Her mother gave a wan smile, and a tug of empathy rose in Allie's chest. She'd never seen her mother wearing red lipstick. Any makeup really. Frying burgers and fries for the tourists that swarmed the town every day wasn't exactly conducive to glamour.

Heartland Cove's main industries were potato farms and lavender fields—and buses that disgorged tourists three times a day to gawk at the Heartland Cove bridge —the world's longest covered bridge.

Mrs. Strickland brushed off any discomfort she was feeling. "I'm a fish out of water in the glamour of Toronto."

"You look lovely, Mom."

Her mother was wearing a maroon sheath trimmed

in lace, black pumps, pantyhose, and a ton of hairspray in a traditional middle-aged pouf. A far cry from jeans and a splattered, greasy apron.

Her cell phone began to buzz, and she recognized the familiar ring of her fiancé. "It's Sean!" she shrieked, patting at her dress and then peering along the floorboard of the car. "I can't find my phone! Why's he calling? I talked to him just before we left the apartment. What if he got in an accident?"

"Calm down," Jake said, speeding through a light. He turned to give Allie a grin. "Knowing him, he's calling about the cop giving him a speeding ticket right about now."

"Be useful and help me find my phone, Erin!"

Her sister pressed her lips together and folded her arms across her chest, tapping one toe on the floor mat.

"Okay, sorry," Allie quickly corrected. "I'm sorry. I don't know why I'm panicking."

"Wedding day jitters," Marla said soothingly, searching under the car seats.

Allie lifted wads of satin as delicately as possible. She shook out the folds of her gown, but there was no sign of the phone. It was as if it had disappeared into another dimension.

"I wish you'd gotten married in Heartland Cove, sweetheart," Mrs. Strickland said wistfully.

The ringing had stopped by now and Allie's stomach

clenched. Sean had trained her to never miss a phone call from anyone.

He always said that if they were going to excel at their careers and strive for every possible promotion, they could open their own law firm one day, Allie as office manager and head of PR. "Let no opportunity go to waste," Sean said. "Grab them all."

"My phone couldn't couldn't have vanished into thin air."

"It's probably on the floor," Erin said with a yawn.

"Can you help me reach down and get it?"

Erin heaved a second deep sigh and dug around the floor, swishing yards of satin and tulle out of her way.

"Careful of my dress!"

"I'm being careful. And . . . it's not here."

"Marla!" Allie said, panic bringing tears to her eyes.

"Don't you dare cry and mess up that makeup job. Here, grab the seat back and lift your bum." Marla ran her fingers along the leather seat under Allie's wedding gown. "Aha!" She held up the cell phone between two fingers and plopped it into Allie's lap.

"You're a lifesaver." Allie quickly checked her voicemail. Sean's deep voice spoke into her ear. "Hey, Allie, I had to run by the office to pick up a new report for this case. Mr. Thompson said I have to read it tonight. The defendant was caught—well, never mind what he was doing. I can't tell you that. But I *will* be at the church. Hitting green lights now, almost to the office."

His voice abruptly stopped and Allie stared at the lifeless phone. It would have been nice to hear an "I love you", but perhaps he'd found a parking space and run inside the office building.

"What's up?" Marla asked.

"Nothing," she lied. "Everything is fine." Inside, she couldn't help fuming. "He might be five minutes late," she added, just to prepare her family.

She hated when they complained about Sean and his awful work schedule. She didn't want to give them any more ammunition than necessary. Sean was there for all the important occasions. Right now was a critical time in his career and when they were able to be together in the same house it would be so much easier to support each other.

"At least your flight isn't until the morning," Erin said, kicking off her tight dress shoes and studying her tanned legs. No doubt, Allie's sister wanted to be at the lake water skiing.

"Sean will be there waiting for Allie with the minister," Marla said reassuringly.

Despite her words, the sick feeling grew in Allie's stomach.

When Marla nudged her, Allie thoughts scattered. In a low voice her friend said, "I know what you're thinking."

"What?" she hissed under her breath, not wanting the

rest of the inhabitants of the car to overhear them; namely her diary-reading younger sister.

"You don't want to be embarrassed if Sean is late because you know Courtney Willis is going to be in the front row of the church, watching you marry her old boyfriend."

"The front row is reserved for family."

"That was supposed to be rhetorical."

Sadly, Allie knew what she meant. "In what universe is it fair that Sean's old girlfriend gets paired up with *my* fiancé on this new high profile case?"

"In the universe of Ally Strickland," Marla said prophetically.

"That is *not* funny."

"I'm trying to get you to crack a smile. You should be glowing. You're marrying the man of your dreams—not Courtney's dreams. She lost him. Bask in the triumph. Hold your head high."

"Why did Sean invite her in the first place? We had two arguments about Courtney over the past month."

"I stamped all your wedding invitations myself. Sean sent one to every employee at the firm. He couldn't leave her out, especially when they're paired up on this case."

"Why did she RSVP? Doesn't she realize that she wasn't actually expected to attend?"

Before Marla could answer, Jake turned off the ignition and jumped out to open the doors all around. "We're here!"

Allie's stomach lurched. The journey to the beautiful little church was over. The moment had arrived.

In forty-five minutes she would be Mrs. Sean Carter.

Grab the rest of THE NEIGHBOR'S SECRET HERE! FREE on Kindle Unlimited!

Caleb Davenport gripped his briefcase, sliding out of the
hired car paid for by the company account. After a

transatlantic flight it was a relief not having to worry about throwing a few twenty dollar bills at the driver, or digging out his credit card. He strode toward the double glass doors of the high-rise club in downtown Denver.

Breathing in the crisp fall air, Caleb finally relaxed, even though he was jet-lagged after making the transfer from Hong Kong via Los Angeles.

He was home, and the Rocky Mountains exuded their own sweet, familiar scent. The high altitude was bracing, clean and fresh. No more stifling hot, crowded streets with a hundred different scents of food vendors, perfumes, and body odor.

Eager to meet up with the rest of the partners of DREAMS, Caleb punched the elevator button for the ninth floor. His stomach grumbled demanding food. Maybe he and the rest of the guys should have met up over dinner. It was later than he'd thought and the small sandwich on the plane hours ago hadn't exactly been filling.

Waiting for his luggage had taken longer than expected, too, and on this particular Friday night Denver's downtown streets were packed with taxis, rental cars, the 16th Street mall shuttle, as well as the Light Rail commuter train coming in and out of the convention center tracks. A couple of buses rumbled past, filled with name tag wearing folks. Must be some big conventions going on this weekend.

Personally, Caleb was convention-ed out. Three of

them back-to-back overseas with more than a dozen companies signing onto the hot new app. His baby, DREAMS; the computer site and app he'd spent years working on.

All in all, the past week had been a resounding success. His little company had grown by leaps and bounds over the past few years, serving thousands of consumers with insanely inexpensive products around the world.

It was mind-blowing to think he was going to bank close to a billion dollars by the end of the year—and it all started with his group of high school computer geek friends.

Caleb's pace turned brisk when he pushed through the glass doors into the posh vestibule of the bar. The five of them; Troy, Brandon, Ryan, Adam, and himself, sent each other a deluge of text messages while overseas —but they often didn't convey many details. Even more often were missing text messages. As if they disappeared traveling through long distance phone lines in third world countries.

The one message that had managed to get through to everyone was his invitation to celebrate at their favorite bar.

"Meet me at *The 54*," he'd texted and, like a ten-thousand-mile miracle from across the Pacific Ocean, he'd received four thumbs up from his partners.

At the end of the plush carpeted vestibule, Caleb

opened the second glass door that spelled out *The 54* in swirly gold letters. He was greeted by the hostess, a woman of about twenty-five dressed in a black dress that shimmered from a luminescent fabric. Sleeveless, plunging neckline, the woman had a terrific figure, and toned arms as if she had an exercise trainer.

"Good evening, sir. Welcome to *The 54,*" she purred in a cultured voice with a slight accent. Italian? English? He couldn't quite detect her country of origin, although he should, he'd been to London and Rome often enough the past few years on business. "Do you have a reservation with us tonight?"

"Reservation's under Caleb Davenport."

The hostess placed a red manicured finger on her wait list. A small lamp on the tall desk illuminating the ledger with a golden glow.

"I have you right here, Mr. Davenport," she said. "Please follow me."

When she sashayed Caleb to his reserved table in the back, he noted the shapely legs in five-inch high stilettos. With the heels, she was still much shorter than Caleb, who, at six feet four often came across as a big, lumbering bear, even while keeping in shape by running five miles every day. She couldn't be more than five feet two. Despite the attractive women he ran into making business deals and traveling, most women were too short for his taste. He'd love a girl who was closer to five foot ten or taller, actually. Someone he could dance cheek-to-cheek with. A woman he could kiss without breaking his back.

Of course, Caleb wasn't planning to hit on *The 54's* hostess, despite her beauty and lovely accent. But once again, whenever he saw a woman he admired, Caleb instantly found himself thinking about the woman he did want. The woman he wanted for his wife and the mother of his children. Someone to share all this—this crazy life—the money—the travel. And yes, the burden.

Having DREAMS thrive so quickly was often disorienting. When he returned home, Caleb had to purposely ground himself by spending time with his best friends. He'd eat at his favorite restaurants, kick-back at home with a Jason Bourne flick, sit outdoors at the Red Rocks Amphitheater for a concert, or take a hike in the pine forests.

And, of course, make a visit to his parents. Despite the pain that visit brought. Tonight he was feeling guilty, knowing he hadn't visited them in nearly a year. It was too difficult, emotionally distracting, and exhausting, but his mother's birthday was coming up and she'd never forgive him if he didn't bring himself bearing a gift.

It might be crazy to make a list of what he wanted in a woman, but when the hostess showed him their table for five and laid out their menus, Caleb realized he could practically reach down and pat her on the head like she was twelve-years-old. Girls who could wear heels and look him in the eye were hard to find, but a definite priority for his "list". Harder to find in the Asian countries he was currently visiting setting up accounts for DREAMS. Idly, Caleb wondered if women were taller in London where Troy usually traveled. He'd have to ask, he thought, and then grinned to himself.

Pushing thirty, Caleb was ready to find *the* woman. A woman he could spend the rest of his life with. His business and travel didn't leave much time for dating. Let alone women he could talk to without an interpreter. Even if they spoke English and he loved their accent, it wasn't the same. Whether it was books or music or movies or favorite foods, they had little in common.

Caleb gave a sigh and dropped his briefcase to the floor by the table, glancing about for any sign of his team.

The 54 was quieter than most upscale Denver club for the rich citizens of this city. And for him, having a membership here was a reality that was hard to calibrate with his old life.

When Caleb stared at the art deco on the walls, the polished 1920s furnishings, and the painted ceilings, he felt like an outsider.

Heck, he'd grown up in a poor neighborhood, attended a passable elementary school, but fortunate that it fed into a better high school. His father had been a drunken mechanic working odd jobs at home, his mother a part-time school aide who kept her husband company at night with the bottle.

At ten years old, he used to dream of buying them a new house one day. A house that wasn't hanging together with duct tape. Mostly because *he* was the one who wanted to escape his depressing life. He never had friends over. Never told anyone where he lived.

Sitting here now in a posh bar was so diametrically opposite to how he'd grown up that his life felt surreal. As if he could blink his eyes and it would all disappear like a dream.

"Hey, buddy, what are you doing here?" a voice came from behind, echoing his thoughts uncannily.

He whipped around to see Troy Thurlow, his best friend since high school, barreling toward him. "Hey yourself."

"They let riffraff in these places now?" Troy teased.

"Nope, I sneaked in. Like usual."

"That's what I figured." Troy plopped into a seat and grabbed the drink menu.

Caleb still had moments where Troy's friendship and their partnership in DREAMS felt bizarre. But the two of them discovered they had a talent for calculus and computers so they'd end up at the Thurlow home doing math homework while watching *Breaking Bad,* and surreptitiously studied the cheerleaders during lunch in the quad.

Caleb was the greasy geek of the school. A loner who

purposely stayed under the radar in the computer lab, except for moments with Troy—when he was virtually invisible next to the vastly more popular football player. There were times during high school that Caleb had wondered if he was Troy's pity project, or a dare. Now he didn't know what he was. Still a geek? Finally grown up when he turned twenty-nine in January?

"Looks like you're overthinking things as usual," Troy said, slapping him on the shoulder.

Caleb gave a snort. "What makes you say that?"

"Your expression was very studious. Bad flight home?"

"Nope, completely uneventful. Just . . . thinking, like you always say."

"It's a woman, isn't it?" Troy gave a grin, waggling his eyebrows. "Who'd you meet in Hong Kong?"

"Nobody," Caleb burst out with a laugh.

"The airline attendant must have been hot then."

Without warning, Brandon appeared and slid into a chair. "You met a babe flight attendant? Tell us more."

Caleb let out a longer laugh. "I couldn't even tell you what the flight attendants looked like. Short? Dark hair? Polite? Served food and drinks. End of story."

Brandon flipped open a menu. "Here I was all ready for a juicy story."

"You mean you didn't meet the woman of your dreams in Brazil, Brandon?" Troy kicked back in his seat and placed his hands behind his head after signaling to the waitress.

"Next time please send me to Rio during Mardi Gras," Brandon told Caleb.

"Nothin' doin'. You'd never come home again."

"There are perks to this job, right?" Troy went on. "But, no, our boss is all work, work, work. I spend the other half of my life sitting on planes."

"Welcome to the real world," Ryan Argyle said, coming up to the table and bumping fists with the rest of the men. Right on his heels was the last member of the DREAMS team, Adam Caldwell, pulling off his tie and unbuttoning the top button of a crisp blue shirt.

"Good, we're finally all here," Caleb said. "Now we can order."

"Hey, I came as soon as I shut down the office," Adam said. "I work longer hours than all of you put together, flying around the world, dancing with luscious foreign women at night."

"Hardly," Troy said with a glance upward at the waitress, a thin woman of about thirty-five wearing black slacks, a black blouse and thick black eyeliner. "I'll have a ginger ale."

The other guys laughed and Caleb held up his hands to ward off their teasing. "A Coke with vanilla," he said. "And keep the nachos coming, please. Mini sliders, too."

"What's with all the fizzy drinks, guys?" Ryan said. "I

know Caleb doesn't touch anything hard, but what about the rest of you guys?"

"Headache," Troy said. "Jet lag is getting to me. I can't even remember what time zone I'm in."

"Mountain Time, poor baby," Adam interjected. "Try sitting at a desk logging orders and shipments until your eyes go numb. I'll have a cold beer, please."

"Didn't know eyes could turn numb," Caleb laughed, giving the youngest member of their crew a teasing grin. Adam Caldwell had been in the class a year behind them in high school. But his computer skills were ferocious so Caleb had hired him two years ago. "That's a new one."

He'd known these guys for so long, but what most of them forgot—except for Troy—was the fact that Caleb never drank. He'd grown up with alcoholic parents and after binge-drinking at a party his senior year, he'd passed out and wouldn't wake up. Terrified, Troy had called an ambulance, afraid Caleb was going to die from alcohol poisoning.

Caleb would never forget his mother speaking at his hospital bedside in a soft voice. "Isn't it bad enough that your father does this?"

She'd been so hurt, her tired face so full of despair, that Caleb hadn't touched a drink since. Despite the teasing during college, the parties going on at his dorm, he just *didn't*. It wasn't worth it. Besides, he wanted to live rather than get a buzz. And avoid liver damage like his father was now suffering with.

Troy ran his hands through his thick dark hair, slouching back in his chair. He was a big man, wide shouldered, with a chest as broad as a football field. Played wide receiver during high school at their alma mater, Southfield High School, but loved the intricacies of computer hardware. He was the guy that could trouble-shoot anything. "Man, it's good to be home."

"Homesick, buddy?" Adam teased.

Troy gave a half smile, shrugging. "There's something about the fall mountain air of Denver that clears your head. South America is just hot and sticky, no matter what time of year you visit."

"Speaking of autumn, what month are we in?" Ryan said, scrolling a thumb across his phone screen. "I've been in too many time zones to remember."

"Months—times zones—it's all the same, oh brainy one," Caleb said, and then added, "Just turned October. We have to hit the office tomorrow, guys. It's only Tuesday and we've got a boatload of data to enter and organize and get on the app."

"Yeah, yeah, we know boss," Troy said, stuffing a burger slider into his mouth now. "You don't have to remind us."

September had proven to be a grueling month and the guys were just doing their usual complaining when they put in an eighty-hour work week during travel but some days he hated being the CEO. They'd known each since their teens, and it often was uncomfortable to be their boss, having to crack the whip with his high school friends.

Ryan dipped a tortilla chip into the nacho cheese dip. "Only asking because I just remembered that we have our ten-year high school reunion later this month."

"We couldn't possibly be that old," Troy quipped, picking up his second slider in under sixty seconds. "Wasn't it only last June that we graduated?"

Ryan gave Troy an eye roll. "Oh, wise one, thank you for that. Did your invitations arrive in the mail? I think it's being held at the Hotel Monaco on Champa Street. Dinner and a DJ, of course. No host bar."

"Ooh, fancy," Adam said. "They must think we're rich."

Low chuckles erupted around the table while Troy said, "Hopefully they don't make us play any stupid games. I'll never forget our senior picnic. Getting dragged in the mud during the tug of war."

"You should have hung on," Caleb teased him.

"If I recall the food was good," Brandon added. "Never-ending barbecue and pie."

"To you, the food is always good," Troy told him. "You have a bottomless pit for a stomach. Your travel reimbursement for restaurants is astronomical."

"Have we made a pact to go—or not?" Ryan asked. "Don't want to show up alone and make small talk with people I don't recognize."

Caleb had forgotten about the reunion, actually. It

wasn't in his planner. He shook the hair out of his eyes and stared around the table. All the guys were gazing at him. Like he was the boss of the high school reunion, too. "We could draw straws," he said with a half smile.

"Better than tossing a coin," Adam said, pulling out his calculator to figure out the odds.

An odd shiver ran through Caleb. Recalling the insane stuff that had happened with his parents during high school still felt surreal. He'd basically been on his own since seventeen, but instead of a fierce independence without having to care about anybody but himself, the opposite had happened.

Traveling the world, making bigger bucks than he could ever have dreamed, had produced a lonely, untethered life. Sure, he could do whatever he wanted, but running a company on which hundreds of employees relied on you in twenty different countries, including a team of accountants and lawyers watching your every move created stress that was also far greater than he could have imagined.

He relied on the men sitting around the dinner table very much. Not just for business, but for friendship and support, saving him from total loneliness. They'd certainly become his surrogate family, and having the support of his friends meant that he avoided obsessing about the past and his derelict parents—except for one person that had never left his memory.

The girl he'd had a crush on since he was a freshman.

English class. Staring at the back of her head like a dunce. Caleb sat two desks behind her, fantasizing about running his hands through the silky strands of her shiny hair that swayed along her shoulders and down her back like a waterfall. Yeah, typical teenage boy stuff.

But that girl was untouchable. Far above his low class life. She was soft-spoken and gentle with a laugh that used to make him smile. She wasn't annoying or loud like most girls in high school, vying for attention or queen bee status. She was perfect. The kind of girl you could fall in love with and live happily ever after—if there was such a thing. Unfortunately, he didn't know many happily ever after's. None of his friends were married. A few of his international clients were happily divorced or living up the bachelor life.

He must be the most peculiar man out there to crave a traditional marriage and family. A house that smelled of fresh baked cookies and filled with people who loved each other and didn't have yelling matches or drunken stupors.

There were a lot of reasons Caleb used to hide out in the computer lab, learning C++. When he created computer games it was like submerging himself under water. He could be immune from the world until the janitor kicked him out.

But *that girl* topped the list of reasons. Seeing her every day made him drown with a desire like a vice squeezing at his heart. Caleb just made sure he didn't drool on his desk.

The most bizarre thing was the fact that he still thought about her. More than ten years later. Images would flash through his mind of her standing at her locker spinning the combination lock. In the cafeteria thoughtfully eating French fries. Bent over a class assignment, scribbling furiously while her satin hair draped her arm.

He'd get up to sharpen a pencil just so he could sneak a peek at her touching the tip of her tongue on her top lip in concentration, erasing a line, rummaging in her purse, or drumming her slender fingers on the desk as if practicing piano scales. Everything about her mesmerized him.

So, the question was, would *she* be at the class reunion?

Caleb gulped down his drink, inwardly shaking his head at his idiocy.

She was probably married and had three kids. Plus, a mortgage and an accountant for a husband in the ritzy suburb of Greenwood Village.

Of course, maybe she'd moved far away, like California, South Dakota, or Florida.

For all he knew, she could be serving as a Red Cross nurse in Africa.

When Caleb discovered the high school reunion

notice in his mail a couple of months ago, fresh hope had lodged firmly in his throat.

"Hey, earth to Caleb, earth to Caleb," Troy said punching him on the arm.

Startled, Caleb knocked over his glass, soda drizzling across the white tablecloth. He grabbed napkins and blotted it out. "Hey, watch it," he joked in an attempt to hide his daydreaming.

"You alright, Mr. Boss?" Ryan said, motioning to the waitress for more napkins and a fresh drink for Caleb.

"I'm fine," Caleb said, glancing around the table at his co-workers. "Never better."

"Jet lag, I tell you," Brandon said. "Especially when you've been in Hong Kong. It's the worst. You lose a day, you gain a day. Over and over again."

Deftly, their waitress served a fresh glass of soda and ice, mopped up the spill, and then scooped up handfuls of soggy napkins.

Adam stared after her retreating figure, obviously wishing he could flirt with her. The guy flirted with every female within ten feet.

"So," Caleb said, glancing around the table. Most of the food was gone, but he dipped a tortilla chip into the last of the salsa with a nonchalant air. "Everybody going to the reunion, then?"

Adam snorted and Ryan cocked an eyebrow. "Yeah, Mr. Boss. Five minutes ago, we decided we were all going together. Stag. It'll give us a chance to check out the girls who broke our hearts ten years ago. Fourteen years for old Troy here since he's been dopey about some girl since his freshman year. Now I call that pathetic."

Caleb gave a forced laugh, hoping the guys hadn't noticed that he'd missed the last thread of the conversation. He reached for the menu, still hungry. "Where's our waitress?"

"You just zoned out," Troy said, staring at him. "We're leaving *The 54* and just waiting for the check. We decided we need real food so we're going to *Rossi's* for dinner. This was just appetizers."

"Okay." Caleb wondered if he could stay awake. "Haven't been to *Rossi's* in ages."

The check came and he stuck his American Express on the plastic plate. The waitress whisked it away and was back again in moments. Caleb scribbled his signature and rose, suddenly needing fresh air.

The other guys filed out noisily, talking, catching up, while Caleb followed, tucking his wallet into his back pocket.

It was only eight o'clock. He'd look like a wimp if he went home without treating the guys to a nice dinner after their ten days of travel. It was a tradition, actually. But man, he was dead tired. What was wrong with him?

A stupid question. It was the class reunion. The thought of it depressed him. He could imagine getting dressed up, making the effort, only to find out *she* was living in a village in Bulgaria teaching English to eight-year-olds.

The October air was brisk, smacking him in the face while they congregated around the taxi circle in front of *The 54.* The bar's sign blared a bright neon blue behind them while they waited for a taxi to come around the block.

Standing just outside the circle of light spilling from the lobby, Caleb surreptitiously reached into his wallet and flipped open the billfold. Tonight's talk had made him nostalgic.

Inside the leather billfold was a small compartment. For years, he'd kept a secret within the small pouch—a dainty chain of silver with a red ruby dangling from the bottom.

He'd kept the necklace with him for almost eleven years. Ever since she'd accidentally dropped it the middle of their senior year and he'd snatched it up.

Caleb didn't take it out very often. The necklace was one part guilty pleasure, the other part pure guilt that he'd never returned it.

While clenching the necklace in his fist, a taxi pulled up and the other four guys piled in, leaving the shot-gun spot free for their CEO.

"Let's hit the road," he heard them call while the vehicle's doors slammed shut and the engine idled, waiting for him.

Caleb slipped the ruby necklace with its two small

diamonds back into the tiny pouch of the billfold, jammed it into his rear pocket, and clenched the handle of his briefcase.

Enough was enough. He had to return it. It was wrong to have kept it. But first he had to find the girl who used to wear it, the red gemstone dangling in the air when she hovered over her math homework in the corner of Algebra class. Far away from him.

Over the years, he'd run into old classmates at the movies, or at restaurants. But never her.

Not that he hadn't made an attempt. He'd looked all right. Her parents were still in the phone book but on a different street than where she had grown up.

But she wasn't listed.

And she wasn't on Facebook.

He was too embarrassed to reach out to her old friends. Or to call her parents.

Even though they'd been in classes together, off and on, she had never given him a second glance. Heck, he would have died and gone to heaven for a first glance, but he'd been a geek in every sense of the word. Frizzy hair. Dorky glasses. Nerdy jeans that never fit properly, bought at second-hand shops, and perpetually hiding his family's secrets from the world.

Years had become a decade.

Caleb gave a snort of self derision. Wow, his lack of confidence when it came to women had become a numbing force that froze him into limbo.

"Where to?" the cab driver asked, pulling into traffic.

"*Rossi's*," Caleb said, noticing how the other guys let him answer. Deferring to him as the boss. It was still odd, even after five years.

Her necklace had become a memento of his stupid high school years, but she was lost to time and distance.

How did you get over a girl you never had in the first place?

A small surge of hope rose up his throat. Would she be at the high school reunion? It might be his only—and last—chance.

Grab the rest of *The Executive's Secret* right here!
FREE on Kindle Unlimited!

Many thanks for reading my novels!
www.KimberleyMontpetit.com

www.ingramcontent.com/pod-product-compliance
Lightning Source LLC
Chambersburg PA
CBHW061422160726
47995CB00003B/716